"Who's there?" Joe asked nervously.

Joe's pulse rate sped up as beads of sweat began to form on his forehead. The drumbeats were coming even faster. Joe's heart seemed to be pounding in time with the rapid beats.

"Who is it?" Joe asked, his voice even more shaky than before. He immediately looked for Wishbone to make sure the dog was nearby. Locating Wishbone just a few feet away, Joe scanned the forest with his flashlight. He hoped the light would land on whoever was beating the drums.

What if there is no one? Joe thought. *What if the drums aren't real drums?* Joe's heart felt as if it would burst out of his chest. *What if it's the ghost of Ka Nowa——*

WHOOOOSH!!!

Joe leaped back as the tiny campfire suddenly exploded. A large blue flame shot high up into the air!

Wishbone
SUPER
Mysteries

THE GHOST OF CAMP KA NOWATO

by Michael Anthony Steele
WISHBONE™ created by Rick Duffield

Big Red Chair Books™, *A Division of **Lyrick** Publishing*™

This book is a work of fiction. The characters, incidents, and dialogues are products of the author's imagination and are not to be construed as real. Any resemblance to actual events or persons, living or dead, is entirely coincidental.

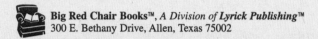 **Big Red Chair Books**™, *A Division of Lyrick Publishing*™
300 E. Bethany Drive, Allen, Texas 75002

Edited by Kevin Ryan

Copy edited by Jonathon Brodman

Cover concept and design by Lyle Miller

Interior illustrations by Al Fiorentino

Wishbone™ photograph by Carol Kaelson

Library of Congress Catalog Card Number: 98-68690

ISBN: 1-57064-970-7

First printing: April 1999

10 9 8 7 6 5 4 3 2

Dedicated to the
George W. Pirtle Scout Reservation
and all who camp there

FROM THE BIG RED CHAIR . . .

Oh . . . hi! Wishbone here. You caught me right in the middle of some of my favorite things—books. Let me welcome you to THE WISHBONE SUPER MYSTERIES. In each story, I help my human friends solve a puzzling mystery. In *THE GHOST OF CAMP KA NOWATO*, my pals, Joe, Sam, and David, and I are helping out at a nearby summer camp. All goes well, at first. Then, strange things begin to happen. Is it true that the camp is haunted?!

This story takes place in early summer, during the same time period as the events that you'll see in the second season of my WISHBONE television show. In this story, Joe is fourteen, and he and his friends are about the enter the ninth grade. Like me, they are always ready for adventure . . . and a good mystery.

You're in for a real treat, so pull up a chair and a snack and sink your teeth into *THE GHOST OF CAMP KA NOWATO!*

Chapter One

"Helllooo, Oakdale!" Wishbone said as he trotted down Oak Street. "You're my kind of town!" The Jack Russell terrier was in a great mood. It was a Saturday afternoon. It was the beginning of summer, and Wishbone was walking with his best friend in the whole world—Joe Talbot.

Wishbone looked ahead at Joe as he followed him along the downtown sidewalk. The fourteen-year-old boy wore denim shorts. His tan T-shirt and short brown hair ruffled lightly in the warm breeze as he continued down the street.

The white-with-brown-and-black-spots dog looked around as he and Joe walked along. The old buildings that lined Oak Street were full of activity. Steady streams of shoppers entered and exited the buildings. Wishbone's sharp ears let him hear the different shop bells ring as all the doors opened and closed. Wishbone thought all the bells together sounded like wind chimes on a breezy day.

7

"What a great day this . . . Hey!" Wishbone quickly jumped to his right to avoid being stepped on. A tall man carrying a large shopping bag walked by. "Excuse me," Wishbone said, looking over his shoulder. The man continued down the sidewalk toward Oakdale Sports & Games. He hadn't even seen The Dog.

That wasn't the first time that had happened that day. Wishbone had already sidestepped a couple of times to avoid people's feet. He wasn't really annoyed, however. The people of Oakdale had just been busy enjoying the great day the same way he had.

Wishbone watched as an older woman quickly walked out of the alleyway between Oakdale Sports & Games and Rosie's Rendezvous. Her car keys jingled as she rummaged through her large purse. She was not looking at the sidewalk below.

Suddenly, Wishbone slammed on his brakes. He stopped short to keep from being stepped on once again. Then Wishbone just missed being kicked by one of her feet.

"Watch out for the dog, will ya?"

Wishbone carefully glanced down the alleyway to make sure no one else was coming. When he saw the coast was clear, he quickly crossed the open area.

"Okay," Wishbone said to himself, "this is getting a little ridiculous." He continued down the sidewalk. "After all, dogs should be able to enjoy—"

A loud noise caused the dog to spin around quickly. Suddenly, Wishbone saw a boy on a skateboard barreling down on him, just a few feet away. The dog barely had time to leap out of the way. The

eight-year-old boy didn't seem to notice Wishbone as he flew down the sidewalk.

A moment later a young girl, wearing a shiny blue safety helmet, quickly zipped along on her board behind her friend. She passed so close to Wishbone that the wind created by her skateboard lightly ruffled the dog's fur.

Wishbone gave a loud bark. "Hey!" he called. "There's a dog trying to walk down the sidewalk and enjoy the beginning of summer here!" Wishbone turned and gazed at the crowded sidewalk behind him. He didn't hear any more skateboards, but a dog could never be too careful.

Wishbone turned and continued slowly down the sidewalk. Okay, so maybe the early summer crowds *were* starting to annoy him just a little bit. He had always been fond of everyone, and every part of Oakdale—well, *almost* everyone. A few cats came to mind. At the moment, however, Wishbone wasn't very happy. No one seemed to be watching out for the dog. Wishbone wasn't expecting everyone to stop what they were doing and step aside when he trotted down the sidewalk. It would have been nice, but he didn't expect it. He *did* want people to do tiny, nice little things, like maybe trying *not* to step on him or run him over with a skateboard!

Ahead of him, Wishbone saw Joe reach the street corner in front of Beck's Grocery. The boy looked both ways, then crossed the street, making his way toward Pepper Pete's Pizza Parlor.

Pizza! There's nothing that cheers up a dog like pizza!

The terrier quickened his pace. Wishbone trotted down the sidewalk until he was slowed by two ladies walking ahead of him. They were walking side by side. They casually showed each other what they had bought that day. Unfortunately, they were also moving very, very slowly.

"Excuse me," Wishbone told them, "hungry dog coming through."

The two ladies continued to move at an extremely slow pace.

"I just want to get by, please," Wishbone added.

The ladies blocked most of the right side of the walk. Wishbone noticed a small gap between them and the street. He could use that space without running into the busy road.

"Passing lane!" Wishbone called out, as he began to make his way around the two women.

The dog had to stop short and quickly hang back to the right side of the sidewalk. A delivery man used the open space to make his way in the opposite direction. The gray-uniformed man was carrying a small package and a clipboard. He flipped through papers on the clipboard as he passed the two slow-moving ladies. It was a good thing Wishbone had seen him. It was clear he wasn't looking out for the dog either.

Wishbone walked slowly behind the ladies. They were still wrapped up in the middle of a shopping conversation. Wishbone looked ahead and across the street, toward Pepper Pete's. Joe had just reached the front door and had turned to look for him.

"Don't worry, Joe!" Wishbone called. "I'm coming!" Once again, the terrier began to pass the two women. This time, a man holding the hand of a little girl blocked his way and walked past. "Or maybe I'm not," Wishbone said, as he ducked back behind the two ladies.

"Doggie!" the little four-year-old girl cried, as she reached for Wishbone. Her father gently pulled her away from the terrier.

"This doggie," Wishbone replied, "is a hungry doggie." He looked toward Pepper Pete's. Joe had just spotted the terrier.

"Come on, Wishbone!" the boy called.

"I'm trying, Joe," Wishbone said, as he looked up at the slow-moving ladies. "Did you hear that, ladies? My boy needs me to get by!" the little dog said. "And so does my stomach!" Wishbone saw no oncoming pedestrian traffic, so he raced around the two women. When he was finally ahead of them, he quickly jumped to the right to avoid another oncoming shopper.

The coast was finally clear. The sidewalk ahead was open enough for Wishbone to run down freely. When he made it to the corner, he looked across the street to see Joe watching him. With his tail wagging, Wishbone began to cross the street.

Honk!!!

Heart pounding, the dog leaped back onto the curb to avoid the approaching car. "Hey!" Wishbone yelled. "This dog is trying to cross the street and get some pizza!" The car drove by. The only reply was a cloud of white smoke that burst from the car's tailpipe. Wishbone coughed as he was surrounded by the car's exhaust. "I hope whoever is driving that car is on the way to a mechanic."

This time, Wishbone looked both ways before crossing the street. Joe waited for him as he trotted across. "You have to be more careful, Wishbone," Joe said, as the dog approached him. "Not everybody is looking out for dogs crossing the street."

"No one is looking out for dogs *at all,* Joe!" Wishbone replied with a bark. Joe opened the door to Pepper Pete's. Wishbone turned and looked back at the busy street. He knew it wasn't true, but he felt as if all of Oakdale had been out to get him that day. The dog loved his hometown, but at the moment it just seemed kind of cold and uncaring.

As Joe entered Pepper Pete's Pizza Parlor, the dog walked in behind him slowly. Wishbone was greeted by the restaurant's familiar scents. Somehow, even the smell of freshly baked pizza wasn't enough to cheer him up after what he had just experienced.

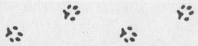

Samantha Kepler set a steaming pizza down on its tray in front of a mother and her two hungry young boys. "Careful, it's hot," she warned, as she placed a small plate in front of each of them. Both boys acted as if they didn't hear Sam's warning. Each grabbed a slice of pizza. They quickly dropped them on their plates and shook the heat off their small fingers. The younger of the two boys put the tips of his fingers in his mouth to cool them off.

Sam gave the boys a smile. She looked to the mother, as if to say "I warned them." The mother smiled back at Sam and shook her head at the impatience of the two kids. "Let me know if you need anything else," Sam added, holding the empty serving tray. "Enjoy your meal."

Sam walked back toward the restaurant's kitchen and set the empty tray on a small table next to the kitchen door. She blew at a strand of long blond hair that had gotten away from her ponytail and hung across her face. Sam brushed it back over her head with one hand. She then looked out toward the tables and booths as she surveyed the pizza parlor.

When her father, Walter Kepler, had first bought the restaurant, it had a very bright, 1950s soda-shop look to it. But after doing a little research, her father had soon discovered that the original owner, Pete Antonelli, had opened the place as a fine Italian restaurant called Antonelli's. So, Sam and her father had decided to decorate the pizza parlor with a combination of both of their ideas. Pepper Pete's still had the juke-box and a few other leftover design elements from the 1950s style. The red-and-white-checked tablecloths and winding-grape murals, however, added a little of "Antonelli's" original charm.

Sam looked at the three tables she was servicing at

the moment. It was mid-afternoon, and the lunch rush was long over. There were only two tables of customers that remained. At one table was the mother and two boys Sam had just served. At another table was a customer Sam knew very well—David Barnes.

She watched as David drank the last sip of his soft drink. His eyes never left the science book he was reading. David Barnes was one those kids who was always trying to learn more about the world around him. Sam was sure he would grow up to be a well-known scientist or a great inventor. She grabbed a cold pitcher of soda and headed over to David's table.

As she walked over, another familiar face entered the restaurant—actually, two familiar faces. Sam saw Joe Talbot enter, followed by his dog, Wishbone. She waved, then walked over to the small table by the kitchen and grabbed a cup for Joe. Sam reached into a napkin-covered basket of bread sticks to get a treat for Wishbone. She then headed back toward the table where David sat.

Joe had always been a good friend of Sam's. He, Sam, and David shared a close friendship. Joe was a trusting and dependable person who also enjoyed going on an adventure or solving a mystery. Actually, all three kids were always ready to try something new and different. With high school coming up when the fall term began, they were all going to get their wish.

"Hey, guys!" Sam said, as Wishbone and Joe joined David at his table. She refilled David's empty cup with soda.

"Hi, Sam," Joe replied, smiling. "Hi, David." Joe

pulled out a chair and sat down. Wishbone sat beside him on the floor.

"Hey, Joe," David remarked. He turned to Sam as he picked up his refilled cup. "Thanks, Sam."

Sam poured Joe a cupful of soft drink and then sat down in the chair beside Wishbone. She handed the dog the bread stick she had been holding. The terrier took it into his mouth carefully and gave a couple of wags of thanks with his tail. It seemed to Sam that Wishbone lacked his usual good-natured spirit.

"How's business?" Joe asked her.

"We had a really big lunch rush," Sam replied. "But everything's pretty quiet now."

"It's really busy outside with shoppers," Joe said. "There's a lot of traffic, too. Wishbone had a little trouble getting across the street." He reached down and gave the dog a couple of pats on the head. "I think he's a bit upset."

Sam looked at the terrier. He was slowly chewing his bread stick. She knew he had to be bothered about something. Usually, Wishbone would be begging for his second bread stick by then.

"Did you go to talk to Mr. Gurney at Rendezvous Books?" David asked Joe. "Is he going to give you another summer job?"

"I went to see him this morning," Joe replied. "I start working the week after next, when Mr. Gurney will be back from his vacation."

"That's great!" Sam said. "As long as you make sure you come here on your lunch breaks."

"You got it," Joe replied.

"What about you, David?" Sam asked the boy,

who had short, curly, dark hair. "What are your summer plans?"

David's eyes lit up with excitement. "Well," he began, "I got an internship to work at Oakdale College!"

"Good news!" Joe said. "What are you going to be doing?"

"I'm not completely sure," David replied. "But I know I'll be assisting Dr. Issacs and his staff in the physics department."

"They certainly picked the right guy for the job," Sam said. "Plus, you told me earlier that you'll get unlimited access to the school observatory and the radio telescope."

David's smile grew wider. "That's the best part!"

"Do you have any special plan in mind, Sam?" Joe asked.

"You're looking at it," Sam replied. "Actually, I'm pretty excited. My dad is going to let me try out some new promotion ideas I've been working on."

"That's good news, Sam," David said.

"Yeah," Joe agreed. "And if you need guinea pigs to try out any new pizza combinations, you know who to call." He looked down and smiled at Wishbone. The dog had finished his bread stick, but he still seemed a bit glum. "I'm sure Wishbone would be happy to help out in that department, as well," Joe added.

Wishbone gave a couple of quick tail wags at the mention of his name, but nothing more. Sam wondered what could be getting him so down.

"Oh, yeah, Tom," a voice said behind them. Sam turned to see her father come out of the kitchen. He was wearing his red apron, and his Pepper Pete's chef's hat was pulled down over his light brown hair. He was holding the store's cordless phone to his ear. "Starting your own business is tough work," her dad continued. "Believe me, I know." His eyes met Sam's, and he gave her a quick wink.

Sam turned back to her friends, David and Joe, to find them watching her father, as well. She turned back to her dad and saw he was looking at the three kids as he spoke.

"Yeah, well . . . about that, Tom," Walter Kepler continued. "What if I told you I might be able to help you in that area?" He paused as Tom replied. "That's right," he answered. "I just might be able to dig up three of them for you. They are here now. Would that help? . . ." He paused again. "Well, I'll have to ask them first. There's no guarantee." Tom replied. "Okay, Tom. I'll call you when I know. Okay. . . . Good-bye."

Her dad took the phone away from his ear and pushed the Off button.

Sam glanced back at the boys. Both of them were still looking toward her dad. David looked at her and shrugged. She looked down at Wishbone, who was also looking toward her dad. The terrier's head was cocked, as if he knew her father had been talking about the kids, as well.

"That was my good friend, Tom Alexander, on the phone," her dad said as he approached their table. The tall man pulled the remaining chair away from the table. He turned it around and sat on it backward. "Tom just bought an old summer camp about forty miles north of town. He's getting a bit of a late start this summer, but he plans on having the camp's first week-long session next week." Her dad looked around the table at the kids, then continued. "He has one problem, though. He's . . . oh, I'd say, about three camp counselors short." Her father looked the kids over once more, then asked, "Would you three be interested?"

Sam looked at the boys. At first, she could see a sign of excitement in their eyes. But the excitement faded and a look of reality appeared. Joe was the first to speak. "That sounds great, but I've already promised Mr. Gurney I'd work for him this summer."

Then David chimed in. "And I've already been accepted as an intern at Oakdale College."

"Well, actually, kids," Walter replied, "Tom only needs someone to fill in for the first week while he puts together the rest of the staff." He gave them a small smile. "You see, the place has been closed for a couple of years. Tom has been trying to fix it up, and he seems to be running a week late with his work. The camp is ready to open, and the campers are scheduled to arrive tomorrow. He just did not have time to hire everyone he needed."

Sam looked around the table and saw the excitement slowly begin to light again in David's and Joe's eyes. "My job with Mr. Gurney doesn't start for more than a week," Joe said quickly.

"If it's only for a week, I might be able to help out," David added.

Sam's father turned to her with a questioning look. Sam didn't wait for the question. "Well," she said, "I have to work here."

Her father leaned over and put an arm around Sam and hugged her to his side. "Well, I know the boss, and I just might be able to arrange for you to get a week off."

Sam knew her dad could see the excitement in her eyes when he had first mentioned the idea. She was just concerned that he really needed her to stay and work. "But what about Pepper Pete's? Don't you need me here?" she asked her father.

"Sam," her dad replied, "of course I need you here. You're a part of this place as much as I am." He hugged her a little tighter. "But you've been working really hard, and you could use a break. I know you would really get a kick out of being a camp counselor for a week." He glanced at the other kids. "Joe and David, I'll call your parents and tell them about the job." He then looked back to Sam. "Besides," he continued, "all of you would be helping out an old friend of mine. I had a lot of friends help me out when I started my own business here. That meant a lot to me. And I'm sure this will mean a lot to Tom."

Sam remembered how hard she and her dad had worked when they'd first bought Pepper Pete's. She also remembered how all of their friends had pitched in and helped in all the chores from the redecorating to handing out flyers on the street. She reached down to pet Wishbone. She smiled as she remembered how even Wishbone had helped by tasting all of their new pizza recipes. The dog wagged his tail and pressed his head against her hand.

Sam looked at the others. "Let's do it!" she said with excitement. "It will be a great way to start off the summer!"

Chapter Two

J oe sat in the front passenger's seat of his mother's forest-green Explorer. He watched the tall evergreen trees zip by in the late Sunday afternoon light. His mother, Ellen Talbot, drove him, David, and Sam to what would be their home for the week—Camp Ka Nowato. He looked back and saw Wishbone sitting in the backseat between Sam and David. The dog's tail wagged when he saw Joe looking at him. He seemed to be in better spirits than he had the day before. Even though Joe and his two friends were staying at the camp for only a week, Joe was going to miss his terrier.

"I bet all three of you will have a great time," Joe's mom said. Joe turned to look at his mother. She was slim and had shoulder-length brown hair. "I went to sleepaway camp a few times when I was a kid."

"I think it's going to be fun. I really like sleepaway camps," Sam added. "Sometimes, when I would spend summers with my mother, I went to an equestrian camp—a camp for horseback riding. I had a great time."

"That sounds really cool," David chimed in. "I've only been to computer camp. That's fun, too, but I'm sure it's completely different from an equestrian camp or Camp Ka Nowato."

"I bet!" Joe responded. "Just a *little* different."

Everyone laughed, and Joe turned his attention back to looking out the window. They had been traveling for about forty minutes down the nearly empty two-lane highway. Joe thought that the farther they traveled, the more civilization seemed to disappear behind them. Both sides of the highway were planted with beautiful green trees. Occasionally, they would pass a house or an old dirt road leading into the woods. But the farther away from Oakdale they drove, the less often he saw even those things. Joe wondered what it would be like to live out there in what seemed like the middle of nowhere.

He thought about Camp Ka Nowato. Unlike Sam and David, Joe had never been to summer camp when he was a kid. So, he felt a bit uneasy about the experience. He looked at the passing trees. The forest seemed so thick and never-ending. Joe couldn't see very far into it. As the sun sank lower in the west, the darker the woods seemed to get.

Joe's mom slowed the vehicle and turned left onto a narrow asphalt road. As she turned, Joe noticed a sign. It read: CAMP KA NOWATO. Below the words, an arrow pointed to the direction of the camp.

The trees seemed to have become even thicker than before. Joe thought it might only seem that way because the road was more narrow. They drove by a few more houses. Then Joe realized the forest actually *was* getting thicker. The farther they traveled down this new road, the narrower it seemed to become. It looked as if the road was poorly maintained. The vines and bushes he saw weren't trimmed back as far as they had been near the road's entrance.

Ellen drove down the road for ten minutes before coming to anything more than just the thick woods. Then, in the distance, Joe noticed that something seemed to be arched over the narrow road. As Joe's mom drove closer to the object, Joe could see clearly that it was a large sign. Written in faded blue letters, it read: WELCOME TO CAMP KA NOWATO. Drawings of feathers and primitive patterns surrounded the lettering. The long sign was hung across the road and held securely in place by two tall totem poles.

The paint on the wooden totem poles was faded, as well. Joe couldn't really make out the different carved animals that were stacked upon one another. He

saw an eagle, or maybe it was a hawk, that sat on top of each pole. The bird's wings were stretched out on each side of the pole. As the group drove under the sign, Joe noticed the two poles appeared to be identical.

As they drove onto what now appeared to be the summer camp's private property, the trees and bushes seemed to reach out for them as they passed. Joe also spotted several smaller totem poles along the way. These less elaborate ones seemed to have only one animal carved into each of them. Joe tried to get a better look as they passed, but most of the small poles were hidden by twisting vines. Joe thought they looked more like something a great explorer would find as he chopped through a thick jungle.

After they had driven about another mile, the road widened briefly and opened up onto a small parking lot ahead. Joe's mom slowed the vehicle as they entered. Joe got his first look at Camp Ka Nowato. The small lot was almost completely surrounded by thick woods. The only open areas were at the road where they came in, and another one leading away at the opposite side of the lot. This probably lead into the main part of the camp.

By the other road stood a small cabin. To their right, two old school buses were parked on the far side of the lot. The buses were a faded blue color. The camp's name was written across them in white letters.

Ellen slowly brought the vehicle to a stop in front of the cabin. As she did, Joe saw a sign in the cabin's window. It read: CAMP OFFICE. The cabin and the buses looked as if they hadn't been used in a long time. In fact, so far Camp Ka Nowato looked kind of creepy.

It had not been a good weekend for Wishbone. The day before, it had seemed as if the entire town of Oakdale had been out to get The Dog. Now, on this Sunday afternoon, Wishbone was going to have to leave Joe and his friends out in the middle of nowhere. After all, who was going to protect his favorite boy?

Everyone opened the Explorer's doors and stepped out. Wishbone quickly hopped out from the opened back door. His paws hit the hard asphalt of the parking lot.

"Well," Wishbone said, as he looked around, "if I have to leave Joe here, I'd better check the place out first."

Wishbone took a couple of deep sniffs. A multitude of scents entered his nostrils. Mostly, Wishbone smelled the sharp aroma of the surrounding pine trees. He smelled the water from the nearby lake, as well as several wild animal scents. There were a few animal smells he didn't recognize, though. Maybe before he and Ellen traveled back to Oakdale, Wishbone could identify a few of the new scents.

As Wishbone looked around the surrounding woods, he felt his worries melt away. The Jack Russell terrier got a strong sense of relief by being in the middle of the woods themselves. There were no crowds of people around to step on him. Wishbone cocked his head and listened. There were no cars honking their horns, no revving engines—no traffic noises at all. He heard only the birds chirping and the light breeze blowing through the trees. The problems of city life were many miles away. *This* was just the way he liked it!

"Is this the right place?" David asked, as he looked around. Hearing David, Wishbone trotted toward the group of his friends.

"This is Camp Ka Nowato, at least the parking lot," Ellen replied. "It just doesn't look very . . . occupied."

As Ellen and the kids looked around what seemed to be a vacant camp, Wishbone looked at the place from a different point of view. At first he had been enjoying the stillness and smells of being far out in the countryside.

Now, as he sensed the uneasiness Joe and everyone else felt, Wishbone slowly looked around at the empty parking lot. Grass and weeds poked up through cracks in the asphalt. Thick weeds grew at the edges of the road entrance and around the base of the old cabin that stood beside the parking lot. The building itself looked as if it could definitely use a fresh coat of paint. Wishbone knew he would never let his *own* coat get so faded and grimy. As the terrier looked into the woods beyond the empty parking lot, something else felt out of place to him. The dog just couldn't quite put his nose on it.

Ellen and the kids walked slowly toward the old office building. Wishbone followed at a distance. Everyone's footsteps seemed to echo across the quiet lot. When they reached the office, Joe reached out for the rusty doorknob. The old door suddenly opened inward. Joe jumped back with a start.

"Whoa!" Wishbone said, also jumping backward.

A young girl came out of the old building. She was followed by a boy who looked a lot like her. They were wearing shorts and matching blue T-shirts. Both of them were about Joe's age, and both had red hair.

"Hey!" Wishbone exclaimed. "Give a dog some warning next time, will ya?"

"I'm sorry we scared you," the girl said with a small giggle. She pushed a long strand of her curly red hair off of her face.

"You just startled me," Joe replied.

The young girl held out her right hand. "My name is Rebecca Williams, and this is my brother, Jeremy." Everyone introduced themselves and shook hands. Rebecca continued: "You must be our temporary camp counselors."

"That's us," Sam said. "My father is Walter Kepler, Mr. Alexander's friend."

"Oh, right," Jeremy replied. A smile crossed his freckle-covered face. "Mr. Alexander was really happy you could come on such short notice." The boy looked toward the road leading away from the camp. "He should be back any time now. He and Barry, the senior counselor, went to pick up the campers."

"*Is* the camp ready to open?" David asked, a bit surprised.

"Yes," Rebecca answered. "Why do you ask?"

"Well, Mr. Kepler did say the camp was ready to open," David said, as he looked around. "It's just that . . ."

Jeremy didn't let him finish. "Trust me, it used to look worse," he said. "We've been fixing up the place for the past two weeks. It's been a pretty hectic time here."

27

Rebecca chimed in. "The place had been vacant for a couple of seasons when Mr. Alexander bought it."

"That's too bad," Ellen said. "I've heard this camp used to be pretty great."

"Well, we're working on it," Jeremy replied. "Would you like a quick tour?"

Everyone agreed. Jeremy took them toward the road that led into the main part of the camp. Before they got to the road, however, Jeremy stopped at a large sign with a roof on it. Wishbone moved in for a closer look. It was a map of Camp Ka Nowato.

The top half, which was north, was painted blue. Wishbone was sure that was supposed to be the lake. The bottom half was completely covered with green, round circles. He thought those were the trees in the forest. There were all kinds of little wooden buildings and other objects glued to the bottom half of the map. They were all connected with little brown lines.

"I'll have to give you the short version," Jeremy said. "I'd take you on a full tour, but we need to stay near the parking lot and wait for Mr. Alexander and the campers."

Wishbone watched as Jeremy pointed out the various objects on the map. He first pointed to a little wooden building glued to a large black square near the right—east—of the sign. Jeremy said the building represented the camp office. Just above that, his finger landed on two miniature totem poles near a brown half circle. Jeremy said this was called the council ring. That was where they would hold their group assemblies.

"It's pretty cool," Rebecca said. "It's like a giant

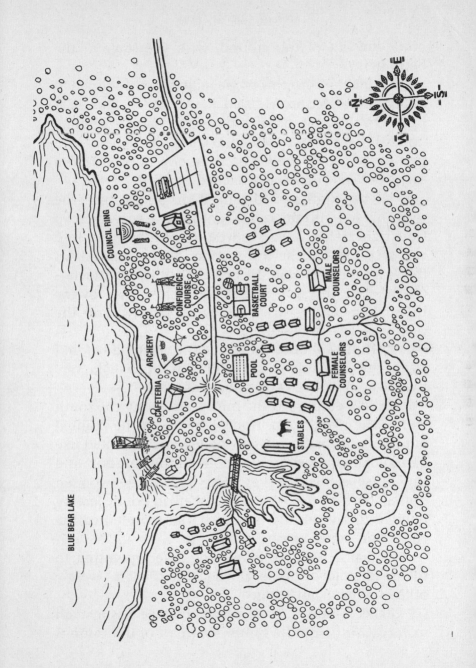

bowl dug out of the ground, with the stage at the bottom."

At the top—north—of the map, Jeremy pointed to a large blue section. He said it was called Blue Bear Lake. On the west, or left side, of the map, Wishbone noticed that the lake seemed to reach a blue hand into part of the camp itself. The little dog noticed that a tiny wooden bridge was stretched across it.

Jeremy continued to name items on the map. The road that led into the camp continued across the map from right to left, or east to west. It split the camp into two sections. On the top section, Jeremy moved his finger from right to left. He pointed out the confidence course—two tiny ropes stretched across two towers; the archery range—a little bow and arrow; and the cafeteria—a large building.

"I think I should check out the cafeteria before I leave, guys," Wishbone said. "I just want to make sure they're going to feed you properly."

Jeremy continued the mini-tour. Along the south end of the road, again, from right to left, he pointed out the basketball court—a wooden circle painted like a basketball; the swimming pool—a little blue box; and the horse stables—represented by a little wooden horse. South of the pool and basketball court, Jeremy pointed to several tiny buildings that represented the counselors' and campers' cabins.

"What's this over here?" Joe asked, pointing to the small group of cabins glued just to the left—west— of the tiny wooden bridge.

Rebecca said, "That's where the lake has a small inlet reaching into the camp. That part of the camp is closed for now, though. The old wooden bridge that crosses the inlet is not very safe." She pointed to the tiny bridge.

"The bridge used to be safe enough," Jeremy said, but Rebecca nudged him to be quiet.

"We won't need to go over there while you're here," Rebecca said to the kids. She pointed to the edge of the lake just above and to the right of the small inlet. Glued to the map at that spot was a tiny little tower and two small canoes. "Here are the docks and the safety tower."

"Safety tower?" David asked curiously.

"It's for watching the campers as they canoe around the lake," Jeremy answered.

"What is this?" Sam pointed to a leaf located on the bottom right side of the map.

"That," Rebecca said as she reached toward the object, "is just a leaf." She brushed it off with one hand. Everyone gave a small chuckle. "I guess it just got stuck to an old piece of glue," Rebecca added.

Wishbone's attention shifted quickly from the map to the parking lot behind him. Actually, his attention shifted *past* the parking lot, to the road leading into camp. The little dog's keen hearing told him two vehicles were approaching.

As the engine sounds got louder, Wishbone glanced back and saw that Joe and the others were now looking toward the camp's parking lot. *Sometimes it takes humans a little longer,* he thought.

Once again, Wishbone turned his attention back to the road leading into the camp. The engine noise had become much louder. Soon a blue school bus appeared. It slowed as it entered the parking lot. Soon after, another bus appeared. It followed the first one in.

These buses looked just like the ones parked on the far side of the lot. The only difference was the fact that these buses had people in them. The sounds of laughing children mixed with the buses' engines. The buses slowly came to a stop in the middle of the parking lot. Wishbone also noticed that the roofs of the buses were loaded with bags, suitcases, and backpacks.

"Come on," Jeremy said, as he motioned to the buses as their drivers parked them. "They're here."

Wishbone, Ellen, and the five kids walked across the pine-needle-covered ground toward the parking lot. As they approached, both of the buses' engines shut off. The buses were both facing toward Wishbone and the others.

In the bus to the right, the driver stood and stepped out. Wishbone saw that he was a tall, thin man who appeared to be in his early forties. His short, dark hair was sprinkled with touches of gray. Wishbone noticed he was wearing a blue T-shirt that matched the one Jeremy and Rebecca were wearing. A smile came across the man's face as he saw the three new kids standing in the parking lot.

"Hey!" the man said. "You must be those lifesavers Walter sent me!" He shifted his attention to Rebecca and Jeremy. "Say, could you two help Barry with the campers?"

"Sure thing," Jeremy said, as he and his sister passed the man and headed toward the buses. Jeremy stepped inside the bus the tall man had just left. Rebecca crossed over to the other bus and joined another adult who was also wearing a blue T-shirt. He had been driving the other bus, so Wishbone thought he was probably Barry. He was shorter than the other driver, and he had short curly hair and dark skin. He appeared to be eighteen or nineteen. Wishbone looked through the windshields of both buses and saw lots of young, excited boys and girls rising from their seats.

"Mr. Alexander?" Joe asked, as the man turned his attention from the two buses.

"That's the name written on my driver's license," he replied with a smile. Then his face froze. Wishbone followed the man's gaze and noticed it had settled on Sam. "Can it be?" Mr. Alexander asked, taking another step closer to the group. "Is that little Sammy?"

Wishbone looked at Sam, who blushed with a little bit of embarrassment. "Hello, Mr. Alexander," she replied.

The man stood there looking at her for a moment, then continued. "The last time I saw you, you were just a little kid, running around and getting into all kinds of mischief." He shook his head. "Obviously I don't visit you and your dad as often as I should."

"That's what he always says," Sam answered with a laugh.

Mr. Alexander stepped up and gave Sam a hug. "You tell your dad I'll try to make it over to Oakdale before you graduate from college." He stepped back and looked at the rest of the group. "Well, Sammy," he said, "who else do we have here?"

Sam turned toward the others. "These are my friends—David Barnes, Joe Talbot, and his mom, Mrs. Talbot," Sam said, as she pointed out each of her companions. Everyone stretched out a hand and greeted Mr. Alexander.

"Hey," Wishbone said, as he hopped straight into the air. "Aren't you forgetting someone!" He hopped up again.

"Did you forget someone?" Mr. Alexander asked, pointing to the leaping dog.

"That's our dog, Wishbone," Ellen said. "He just rode up with me to drop off the kids."

Mr. Alexander knelt in front of Wishbone and held out a hand. "Hello, there, pooch."

Wishbone placed a paw into the man's hand. "Uh . . . no offense, but the name is *Wishbone*, not *pooch*," the dog said with a bark.

"Would you like to work at my summer camp, too?" Mr. Alexander asked the dog.

"Would I!" Wishbone said excitedly with a quick bark.

"I'd sure like to have you here, if it's okay with Joe and Mrs. Talbot, here." Mr. Alexander looked up at them. "I sure could use a first-rate guard dog for a full week."

"A guard dog!" Wishbone exclaimed. "Back home, I'm a great guard dog!" The terrier sat back proudly on his haunches. "You know, those cats don't run *themselves* out of the yard!"

"Okay," Ellen said. She turned to Joe and said, "Just make sure you look out for him, and be sure he doesn't get into trouble. And he'll need some food."

"You just tell me what kind he likes, and I'll send Barry into town for it later," Mr. Alexander said. He gave Wishbone a pat on the head, then stood up. He turned to his new counselors. "Well, why don't you kids unload your gear?" Then he pointed to the kids who were beginning to get off the buses. "Then help the campers unload their gear."

Ellen and the three kids headed toward her sport utility vehicle, while Mr. Alexander made his way toward the two buses. Young children were pouring out of the two old vehicles. Rebecca, Jeremy, and Barry were doing their best to organize the campers.

This is going to be a great experience! Wishbone thought. He would have an entire week away from civilization! The dog would get back to nature. He would live the way his ancient ancestors lived, in a time when mighty packs of Jack Russell terriers roamed the open plains! However, if Wishbone had known he was going to be staying over, he would have brought along his favorite, chewable, book-shaped squeaky toy. Now, he would have to go for a whole week without squeaky! *Oh, well,* Wishbone thought, *I guess that is what people call "roughing it."*

Wishbone was about to join Mr. Alexander and the others, when he suddenly heard a strange noise. It sounded like a rustling noise coming from the woods to his right. Wishbone turned and peered into the thick forest. He supposed the sound wasn't *that* unusual. After all, there were bound to be many different animals living in the surrounding forest. It wouldn't hurt to check out the noise, though. *That's what guard dogs are for!* Wishbone thought.

Wishbone took a couple of steps toward the spot in the woods where he thought he had heard the sound. The terrier lifted his nose into the air and took in a couple of quick sniffs. He trotted a little bit closer toward the trees, but he no longer heard, saw, or smelled anything.

Wishbone decided that the sound must have come from one of the forest's many creatures. He relaxed and trotted back toward the buses. Besides, the terrier thought, the idea of something hiding quietly in the woods and watching them didn't appeal to him at all. Before he reached the rest of the campers, however, Wishbone took one more look over his shoulder at the thick woods.

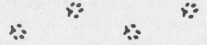

Hidden behind a thick cover of leaves, something watched as the young children filed out of the two buses. It watched as the tall man and the group of older kids began to unload bags and suitcases from the blue vehicles. It also watched as the dog walked slowly toward the trees from where it was watching. The dog had come so close. It had

been just a few feet away. But the dog didn't detect anything, and it had walked back to join the others with only a final look over its shoulder. The watcher continued to secretly observe the people in the parking lot.

Chapter Three

J oe watched as Ellen drove out of the camp's parking lot. He then turned his attention back to the young campers. Sam and David had already walked over to the groups of kids. They seemed much more at ease with the kids than Joe did. Joe actually was nervous. Nevertheless, he tried to put his concerns behind him. He and Wishbone approached the youngsters. When they were a few feet away from the campers, a young girl walked up to Joe.

"I can't find my suitcase," she said. Then she knelt to pet Wishbone.

"Well . . ." Joe started to answer, but was quickly interrupted by another camper.

"What are we going to do all week?" the young boy asked. He looked around the camp. "This place looks too old to be any fun."

"Well, you see . . ." Joe began again. He stopped talking when he felt a tug on his shirtsleeve. He looked down to see another little girl.

"Where are we going to sleep?" she asked.

Joe didn't know what to say. He had just arrived himself. Now, suddenly, he was surrounded by kids who were looking to him for answers.

"Uh . . ." Joe hesitated. He was speechless.

Joe was nervous about being a camp counselor. Without camp experience, he didn't know what to expect. Now, suddenly he was a summer camp counselor. Wasn't a counselor supposed to be more experienced than the campers?

"Hey, everybody!" a loud voice said. Joe turned to see Mr. Alexander waving his hands in the air. "Now, first we're going to get everyone's gear off of the buses. Then we're going to get everyone settled in their cabins. Once that is completed, we'll regroup in the cafeteria for a quick bite to eat." The man had a broad smile on his face. "By the way, welcome to Camp Ka Nowato."

That was all the three kids needed to hear. The campers standing around Joe returned to the crowd at the buses to wait for their gear to be unloaded. Like Joe, they were in a strange, new place. The three campers just seemed to be nervous and in need of a little reassurance. Joe only wished it was that easy for him.

For the next hour, all the young campers and the counselors got settled in their cabins and unpacked their gear. Then they went to the cafeteria for sandwiches. Everyone then gathered at the camp's council ring.

Joe sat down on a wooden bench. Wishbone hopped up next to him. The sun had set completely, but a bit of light still shone from the western sky. Joe looked around at the campers and the rest of the counselors as they gathered inside the council ring.

The ring was like a little outdoor theater. The ground sloped like a large half bowl. At the top of the bowl were rows of wooden benches that were arranged on one side in a semicircle. Toward the bottom of the bowl was a small wooden stage. Immediately behind the stage was a raised stone platform. On top of the platform a small fire was burning. Behind the platform, the ground continued to slope until it reached the lake—the bottom of the bowl.

Blue Bear Lake was a natural backdrop for the stage. The last weak rays of the setting sun made its rippling waters sparkle. Joe turned and glanced over his shoulder. There were still a few campers entering the council ring. He noticed that David was ushering in a small group.

Joe's attention was drawn to his side when Wishbone nudged his hand with his nose. Joe gave the terrier a scratch behind the ears. Joe was glad Mr. Alexander had asked Wishbone to stay on for the week, as well. Although Joe didn't know why, having his pal there made him a little more at ease.

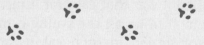

Wishbone watched as David led the last group of kids to join everyone already in the council ring. The terrier was having a great time. He had helped the counselors get all of the campers settled into their cabins. He also got to explore the camp a bit. The place was full of all kinds of fascinating sights and smells.

The first assignment for a first-rate guard dog was to know the turf he was guarding. Wishbone knew he had a very important job to do. But he also knew he was going to have a great time doing it.

Wishbone turned his attention back to the kids around him. Once everyone had sat down, Jeremy and Rebecca walked together down each of the two aisles that cut through the rows of benches. The brother and sister split up and made their way to either side of the stage. They went behind the stage and pulled out two large drums and mallets. With the help of the dancing firelight, Wishbone could see Native American symbols and designs painted on each of the drums. Jeremy and Rebecca looked at each other, then began to beat the drums with quick, synchronized beats.

When the drums sounded, all the campers stopped their casual conversations and turned their attention to the stage. From behind him, Wishbone heard a jingling noise. He turned and looked for the source of the sound.

Walking down one of the aisles that led down the slope was someone who looked like a Native American chief. The man was dressed in light brown buckskin. Many small strips of leather were wound around his arms and legs. The ends of the strips waved in the evening breeze as he walked. The man wore a very large headdress full of long white feathers. A chest plate of long beads and bones hung from his neck. The jingling sound Wishbone had heard was coming from several small bells attached to different parts of the man's costume. The terrier quickly recognized the Native American "chief" as Tom Alexander.

41

To the beat of the two drums, Mr. Alexander continued down the aisle and finally stepped onto the stage. He turned and faced the audience, then raised his arms in a halting motion. When he did, Jeremy and Rebecca stopped beating the drums.

"Welcome, young campers," Mr. Alexander began in a deep, booming voice. "Welcome to Camp Ka Nowato!" The camp owner put his arms down and continued. "Before you sleep under Camp Ka Nowato's stars, you must know its history."

Mr. Alexander raised one arm and pointed with his hand to the surrounding woods.

"Many years ago," he began, his arm swinging around in a large semicircle, "all the land here was owned by a great tribe of Native Americans known as the Chitowa." Mr. Alexander dropped his arm to his side. "The Chitowa were a great and mighty people. They lived in harmony with everything you see—from the pure waters of Blue Bear Lake to the many animals that inhabit the surrounding forest."

Mr. Alexander gave a dramatic pause, then continued.

"But as other Native American tribes were driven off their land, so, too, were the Chitowa. All of the tribespeople were forced to leave their land—all of them but one."

There was another short pause.

"The Chitowa people left behind one of their greatest warriors to guard their sacred burial grounds. The warrior's name was Ka Nowato." When Mr. Alexander spoke the name, he passed one hand high over his head, as if he were spreading the warrior's

42

name across the sky. He then continued. "The warrior's name means 'Watching Dog.'"

What a great name! Wishbone thought. *Ka Nowato was a guard dog, just like me!*

Mr. Alexander continued. "Hundreds of years later, this summer camp was built directly on top of the Chitowas' sacred burial grounds." A brief murmur passed through the audience. Mr. Alexander went on, his voice growing louder and louder. "And, to this day, this land is haunted by the ghost of Ka Nowato!"

Mr. Alexander raised both arms quickly. Behind him, a thick column of smoke rose from the fire. It created a large mushroom as it rose into the early-evening air. The audience gasped. Even Wishbone wasn't ready for that surprise.

"Hey!" the terrier exclaimed. "No one said anything before about this place being haunted!" He put a paw on Joe's leg. "Did you see that, buddy?" Wishbone asked. "Do you think it's too late to have Ellen come pick us up?"

Joe ran a hand across the dog's head. It felt comforting, but only a little.

Mr. Alexander slowly lowered his arms as he continued to tell his story. "Yes, the spirit of Ka Nowato watches over this land. Some have seen him appear in the form of a deer, an owl, or a fox. Others say he's in the blowing breeze, the rippling water of the lake, and the burning fire."

The camp owner's voice lowered a bit.

"Some have even seen him in human form, walking through the woods."

Wishbone felt the tension level of the audience rise a bit more.

"No matter what form Ka Nowato takes," Mr. Alexander said, "the ghost of Ka Nowato will harm no one who respects the land the way his tribespeople did."

"Well, that sure makes me feel better," Wishbone said, as he wagged his tail a few times. "This is one dog that doesn't mess with Mother Nature!" Wishbone loved ghost stories, and that had been a great one. It had a watchdog in it, and much more! Ka Nowato was a watchdog, just the way Wishbone was! Wishbone planned on doing such a great job with his new duties that Ka Nowato would be proud.

After telling his story, Mr. Alexander lightened up the mood of his speech. He welcomed everyone to camp again, and then he introduced the new counselors. Wishbone watched as each of his friends—Joe, David, and Sam—stood when Mr. Alexander announced their names. Each of them wore a light blue T-shirt like the other counselors had on.

The camp owner then introduced the other counselors: Jeremy, Rebecca, and Barry. The brother and sister had already returned to their seats in the audience, but they stood when their names were called. When Mr. Alexander introduced Barry Smith, the older boy stood from his seat at the back of the audience.

After the introductions were over, Mr. Alexander made a few more announcements. Then he joked with a few of the campers and led the group in some songs. Wishbone and everyone else seemed to have a great time!

After the songs, Mr. Alexander said a general good-night to the entire camp. The campers divided up into groups, and each of the counselors began to lead them back to their assigned cabins.

Wishbone decided to make a few guard-dog rounds. *You can never start guarding too early*, he thought. *Besides, after a few hundred years, I bet Ka Nowato would appreciate a little help.*

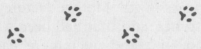

David walked behind a group of boys. They were all about ten years old. They were the oldest age group in the camp. Along the way, David had discovered many of them had an interest in computers, as he did. That really helped break the ice.

Actually, David wished Camp Ka Nowato was a computer camp, like the other ones he had attended as a camper. If that were the case, he felt he could make a larger contribution at Camp Ka Nowato. Here, he had been placed in charge of teaching swimming. It was not an assignment he could not handle. David was a very good swimmer. He had even taken some lifesaving classes and had earned a special certification. David felt he would do the job just fine for the week he was at camp.

Luckily for Sam and Joe, they had been put in charge of tasks more suited for them. Joe was going to teach basketball, definitely his best sport, and Sam was going to be in charge of horseback riding. She had really been excited about that. Apparently, with the experience she had gained from attending equestrian camps in the past, she was very qualified for the current job.

Joe, David, and Sam had filled the only counselor positions that had been left. Rebecca was put in charge of the archery range. Jeremy was put in charge of canoeing. That left just Mr. Alexander and Barry. Mr. Alexander would handle all the administrative tasks and help with the campers as much as he could. However, he had told the counselors that he would be spending most of his time trying to hire permanent staff members.

Barry, on the other hand, was going to take up all the slack. The senior counselor was going to continue to repair and restore the camp, as well as be in charge of the confidence course and the cafeteria. The job of cafeteria assistant was something all the counselors would take turns doing.

David led his group south down the first of three trails leading toward the cabins. The sounds of nighttime in the forest rang in David's ears. To David, the insects' chirping made the forest seem very alive.

The dark woods were illuminated only by the campers' flashlights. All the boys carried flashlights and pointed them toward anything and everything they thought was interesting. The passing trees were lit up by soft, bright circles of light. Up ahead, David saw Jeremy leading a group down the same trail. He, too, walked among what seemed like large, dancing fireflies.

Soon, a bright light glowed in the distance as they approached the boys' cabins. Although the trail was dark, a lamppost stood outside the group of cabins, and its bright bulb lit the immediate area. David and the kids turned off their flashlights as they approached the cabins. They were large, one-room cabins that could house five kids each. David's group split up, and each one went to the cabin they had been assigned to earlier. David made sure everyone was settled in. Then he continued on the trail toward the cabin he shared with Joe, Barry, Jeremy, and Wishbone.

As he walked away from the light shed by the lamppost, he heard a rustling noise ahead of him. David hadn't turned on his flashlight yet, so the trail ahead was dark. Feeling a little nervous, David fumbled for the switch. The rustling grew louder and louder, as if something was approaching—fast. The noise didn't sound like a person's footsteps. It sounded like some sort of animal. David found the flashlight's switch and aimed a bright beam down the trail. His light landed on a white object headed right for him! For a brief moment, David didn't recognize what it was. Then the white blur stepped farther into David's flashlight beam.

"Wishbone!" David said, a bit embarrassed. "What are you doing?"

The dog wagged his tail when he heard his name.

He stopped in front of David, who knelt to pet him. After stroking the terrier's head several times, David felt more at ease.

"You startled me a little," David told the dog. "I didn't know if you were a wild animal." Wishbone let out a small bark, as if offended. David scratched him behind the ears. "Well, it's a good thing you are *our* wild animal. Let's head to our cabin."

David stood and continued on the path leading to the counselors' cabin. He was more comfortable with Wishbone walking at his side. The wooded trails could be pretty creepy at night. He glanced at the dog again and smiled. The woods were even creepier when you were alone.

David supposed Mr. Alexander's ghost story was partly responsible for his feeling of jumpiness at the moment. David wasn't the type of person who believed in ghosts. Yet, sometimes it was fun to let himself get wrapped up in a story. That was just what he had done with Mr. Alexander's story of the ghost of Ka Nowato. After all, it was a good tale. It told the campers to respect the forest. The story had a good moral, even if it wasn't true.

David also knew that the smoke billowing from the campfire was not a ghostly occurrence. He could think of a number of chemical compounds that would create a similar effect. In fact, any fireworks company would carry them in its inventory.

After the smoke had mushroomed up over the ceremonial fire, David had quickly scanned the area for the mechanical tricks behind the illusion. After the smoke had cleared, David looked high into the trees, above the fire, to see a dark object there. No doubt it had been a container holding the compound that had been dropped into the flames.

Another quick look attracted his attention to Jeremy, who had been beating one of the ceremonial drums using only one hand. David had seen Jeremy's other hand carefully come out from behind his back. David was sure that he had pulled some sort of string or wire. The wire would have released whatever had fallen into the fire from above. It was a clever trick, and it had been pulled off very well. No one would have noticed how it had been done . . . well, not unless he or she had really been looking very carefully. David had really been looking carefully.

David and Wishbone walked down the trail until the glow was visible from their cabin. The terrier took off ahead of David. Wishbone ran down the trail and then trotted through the cabin's open doorway.

David was just about to turn off his flashlight when he thought of the camp legend again. Although he didn't believe in ghosts and thought the idea of a spirit running around and watching everyone was silly, he still felt a bit tense. He shone his flashlight into the dark woods on each side of him. It would be easy for anyone to hide in those trees and watch everything that happened around camp. David stopped walking and continued to scan the forest with his light.

Actually, someone could be watching David right then and there. And, since there were so many trees and bushes around, David wouldn't notice he was being spied upon. He let his light beam roam across a few more trees. He didn't see any sign of anyone watching him. David shook his head and continued down the trail. He really didn't believe in ghosts. Nevertheless, he left his flashlight on until he was well under the light of the cabin's lamppost.

Joe stood over the small wooden bed unpacking the gym bag in which he had packed a full week's worth of clothes. He had been so busy getting his assigned campers settled, it wasn't until then that he had time to unpack. It had been a busy evening. He was definitely going to sleep soundly tonight.

Joe looked around his cabin. The two counselors' cabins were a bit bigger than the campers' cabins were. Each of the counselors' cabins could accommodate eight people instead of five. The beds were placed down the length of the cabin in two rows of four. Each bed's head rested against one of the two long walls. A hanging, shaded lightbulb was set over each bed. Each bed also had its own storage cabinet attached to the wall behind it. Joe placed the last of his clothes into the cabinet and then shut the doors.

As Joe placed the empty gym bag under his bed, Wishbone entered the cabin through the open doorway. "Hey, buddy," Joe said, as his dog hopped onto his bed. Wishbone's tail wagged in reply as Joe gave the dog a couple of pats on the back.

Joe's feeling of nervousness about being at camp hadn't really gone away. He was also uneasy about living in the woods, in the middle of nowhere, for an entire week. Mr. Alexander's story about the ghost hadn't helped matters either. Before coming to camp, Joe thought he had gotten past his superstitious nature. Now, he wasn't so sure. The idea that a ghost was lurking around the camp and watching everybody gave Joe the creeps. He tried to let the logical part of his mind to convince him there were no such things as ghosts. Unfortunately, his logical mind seemed to be fighting a losing battle.

David entered the cabin. He turned off his flashlight and threw it onto his bed. Joe felt as if he and David were being housed in an army barracks. Although they were also sharing the cabin with Jeremy and Barry, Joe was glad David chose the bed next to his. The cabin appeared empty and lonely with only four people.

"What do you think so far?" David asked Joe.

"It's going to be an interesting week," Joe replied, trying not to let the doubt show in his voice.

"I think it's going to be fun," David said. "That is, of course, if I can go a whole week without my computer." The two boys laughed as Joe watched David begin to unpack his suitcase.

Joe figured that Jeremy was still with a group of campers. Barry was probably making some last-minute food preparations for tomorrow's breakfast. Joe reached for the small black bag sitting on his bed. It was the only item he hadn't put away in his cabinet. In it, he carried his toothbrush, soap, and other items. He was planning to brush his teeth before going to sleep.

With Wishbone close at his heels, Joe grabbed his bag. He stepped out of the cabin and left David to unpack. As he walked through the night air to where the bathrooms and showers were located, he thought about what Jeremy had said about the old bridge. Jeremy had said it *used* to be safe. That implied that something had since made it *unsafe*. That alone wouldn't have been such a mystery. However, when Rebecca nudged him and then changed the subject, that *did* seem strange. Joe wondered what it was that Rebecca didn't want Jeremy to say.

Wishbone followed Joe and then gave his pal a gruff little bark. Then the terrier headed toward the girls' side of the camp. Joe supposed Wishbone hadn't finished checking up on everybody.

"Don't be too long, Wishbone," Joe said to the newly appointed camp guard dog as he disappeared down the dark trail. Joe really wasn't worried about Wishbone being alone in the dark woods. He could see and smell better than any of the humans there.

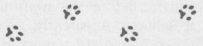

Sam pulled her hair back into a ponytail as she got ready for bed. She and Rebecca had just returned from the young girl campers' cabins. There weren't as many kids attending camp as she thought there would be. Still, Sam had a feeling she and the other counselors would stay busy anyway.

Although Camp Ka Nowato wasn't quite what she had expected, Sam believed she was going to have a good time—a nice mini-vacation from her job at Pepper Pete's. She looked around at the inside of the large cabin only she and Rebecca were sharing. The two counselors' cabins were identical. The two girls had chosen the first two beds. The remaining six sat empty.

In a lot of ways, that was how the whole camp had felt. They hadn't seen much of it before it had gotten dark, but what they had looked at seemed creepy— like a ghost town.

Actually, Sam enjoyed the eerie feeling of the camp. She had always been the type of person who enjoyed spooky places, and Camp Ka Nowato definitely qualified as spooky. The camp's ghost story was also a nice added touch. Sam felt this "haunted camp" would be a pleasant change from the ordinary camps she had attended in the past.

Sam reached over her head and felt around inside the open storage cabinet. After a short search, her hand felt what she was looking for. She pulled down the book she had brought along to read. Sam enjoyed reading each night before she went to sleep. She looked over at Rebecca. Apparently, Rebecca felt the same way. The red-haired girl was wearing glasses as she curled up with a book as well.

Samantha bunched her pillow up behind her back and leaned against the wall at the head of her bed. She was about to open her book when she heard a soft scratching on the door of her cabin.

Rebecca looked up. "What was that?" she asked.

Both girls looked toward the cabin door. Sam enjoyed the sudden tension in the air. Then, Sam realized what it had to be. "I think I have an idea," she said, as she got off her bed and walked toward the door.

Rebecca seemed nervous as Sam turned the doorknob. Sam gave her a reassuring smile, then looked

down to the bottom of the door. When she opened the door, in trotted Wishbone. Rebecca let out a laugh, then turned her attention back to her book.

"It's our resident guard dog making his rounds," Sam said jokingly. "Is everything checking out, Wishbone?"

The dog wagged his tail as Sam returned to her bed. Wishbone jumped up onto the foot of the bed. Sam picked up the book and gave Wishbone a scratch behind the ears.

The book was an old paperback mystery novel. It was called *A Caribbean Mystery*. The novel was written by the famous British mystery author Agatha Christie, and it had originally been published in 1964. Agatha Christie was one of those authors who liked to use the same characters in many different stories and novels. One of these characters was an elderly lady named

Miss Jane Marple. Miss Marple was the main character in *A Caribbean Mystery*.

Like Sam, Miss Marple was also on vacation in a new and different place. Miss Marple had traveled from her home in England to an island resort called the Golden Palm Hotel, in the exotic location of St. Honoré, somewhere in the West Indies. The West Indies was a chain of tropical islands separating the Caribbean Sea from the Atlantic Ocean. Miss Marple's situation mirrored Sam's in another way. The Golden Palm Hotel also had a new owner—or owners. A very pleasant husband-and-wife team named Tim and Molly Kendal ran the place.

When the story began, Miss Marple was sitting on the hotel's terrace reading a book in the fresh sea air. Sitting with her was an elderly gentleman by the name of Major Palgrave. Major Palgrave told her story after story about the time he had spent overseas, away from England. With each story, the major produced an old photograph out of his wallet. He talked about and showed her photos of lions, elephants, and all sorts of other interesting things. He even mentioned how once, while on a safari, he had lost one of his eyes. He had then gotten a glass eye to take its place.

Miss Marple was only half-listening to the man as she politely nodded and agreed occasionally. Soon, the major's conversation turned to a police case in which a man had murdered his wife. He asked Miss Marple if she would like to see a picture of the murderer.

Miss Marple agreed, and Major Palgrave reached into his wallet to take out the photo. He pulled out the picture, glanced at it, then looked at something over

Miss Marple's shoulder. Then Major Palgrave quickly returned the photo to his wallet and began to talk about something else.

Miss Marple found his reaction very strange. She looked over her shoulder and saw that four of the hotel's other guests had come out onto the terrace. Major Palgrave quickly went to them and introduced Miss Marple to them. Miss Marple felt the entire event was quite odd.

Sam stopped reading and watched as Wishbone wagged his tail and jumped off of the bed. The dog trotted over to her cabin door. "I think you have the right idea, Wishbone," Sam said, as she got out of bed and opened the door for the terrier. "It's time to get to sleep."

"Yes, we'd better," Rebecca agreed, as she put her book away. "Mr. Alexander is going to expect us to be up at daybreak." She took off her glasses and pulled the string that was fastened to the light above her bed. The light went off with a click.

Wishbone sat up on his haunches as Sam gave him one more scratch. "Good night, Wishbone," she said, as the dog wagged his tail and took off toward the boys' cabin.

Sam stepped outside and picked up a dried-up brown leaf from the ground. She then went back inside the cabin, closing the door behind her. The young girl returned to her bed and picked up the Agatha Christie book. She used the leaf as a bookmark and placed it onto the page where she had stopped reading.

After placing the book back on the shelf in the cabinet, Sam crawled into bed. She turned off her overhead light. Sam was delighted that after reading only a few pages of her book, something peculiar had already happened. She would have to wait until tomorrow night to find out what would occur next. As for tomorrow, it would be the first full day when she would serve as a counselor at summer camp.

Chapter Four

Wishbone had just finished a nice breakfast in the camp's unusual cafeteria. He had enjoyed eating in the great outdoors, far away from civilization. What more could a dog want?

After breakfast, Wishbone had decided to extend his guard duties and watch over the kitchen cleanup. Barry had cooked, and it was Rebecca's turn to help in the cafeteria. Actually, the cafeteria was a pavilion, or an open structure. There were no walls of any kind. A large wooden roof was supported by a number of large posts. A dozen picnic tables were scattered over a concrete slab that was the pavilion's floor.

The cafeteria's "kitchen" was actually a large outdoor gas grill. Beside the grill were sinks and counter space. Behind the grill, there were two large storage lockers for the food. Both of them seemed newer than the rest of the camp. One was made of sheet metal, while the other was like a giant walk-in refrigerator. It had thick insulated walls, and a motor hummed on top of it.

Wishbone had also given the storage lockers a thorough investigation. *Hey, a good guard dog needs to know his entire territory,* the dog thought. *And if there are any food scraps to dispose of, a great guard dog would be happy to help!*

After everything in the cafeteria checked out, Wishbone trotted west. It was a cool Monday morning. The refreshing breeze from the lake blew through the dog's fur. Wishbone thought it was a wonderful day. He headed toward the docks at the lake, where the canoes were stored. When he was almost there, the trail led to a small hill.

As Wishbone stood on top of the hill, he saw the three short piers. The two on the left were regular wooden docks that extended out over the lake's rippling waters. The third dock, on the far right, was the same as the others, except for one thing. On the end of the pier stood a small tower. It looked like one of the campers' cabins, except it was smaller and stood on four tall wooden stilts. There was an open doorway facing inland. Long, slender, open windows were on its other three sides. A ladder extended from the dock to the tower's doorway. Wishbone thought it must be the safety tower Jeremy had been talking about.

A voice drew Wishbone's attention away from the safety tower. Jeremy held a canoe paddle and stood in front of a group of ten kids. They all sat on benches and watched the counselor as he demonstrated how to paddle a canoe correctly. Behind Jeremy, large wooden racks held several upside-down canoes.

Wishbone thought it would be nice to have Jeremy take him canoeing before the week was over.

As for now, though, Wishbone had the rest of the camp to check out. His guard-dog duties came first.

The terrier ran south along the trail toward the horse stables. Long before he actually saw the stables, Wishbone recognized the familiar smell of horses.

The terrier walked into a large clearing in the woods that surrounded the stables. A long wooden building was surrounded by a large wooden fence. The fence ran completely around the clearing to form a large corral. Wishbone thought it was about a quarter of the size of a football field.

Wishbone trotted up to the wooden fence and put his two front paws on the bottom rung. He saw Sam standing beside a large white-and-brown-spotted horse. Mr. Alexander had said that one's name was Scout. Standing around Sam and Scout were eight boys and girls. Sam was demonstrating how to place the bridle on the horse.

Wishbone glanced at the long wooden building on the other side of the large corral. A smaller white horse stood in one of the stable's many stalls. His name was Silver. The stable had six different stalls, but there were only two horses. Wishbone wondered if Mr. Alexander had the same trouble getting horses as he did getting camp counselors. Maybe later in the summer Mr. Alexander would be able to get Scout and Silver some friends.

The dog hopped down from the fence and walked back the way he had come. Everything checked out at the stables. Besides, a big rule for dogs was never to play around animals big enough to step on them. That ruled out horses, cows, and Great Danes.

The next stop for Wishbone was the pool. As was the case with the stables, the swimming pool was located in a large clearing in the pine forest. Like the stables, Wishbone could smell the pool before he saw it. As he approached, the sharp smell of chlorine entered his nose. He could also hear several small children laughing and splashing.

When he got to the pool, Wishbone put his two front paws up on the chain-link fence that surrounded it. He saw David standing at the pool's edge directing what looked like a relay race. Several youngsters were swimming from one end of the long pool to the other. Everyone looked as if they were having a great time.

Wishbone made his way north, up the trail, and onto the main road. He continued east until he reached the trail that led to the archery range. The terrier took a left as he proceeded up the narrow trail.

Unlike his experience when he had approached the stables and the swimming pool, Wishbone didn't smell the archery range before he saw it. He did, however, hear it. The dog heard the whiplike sound of arrows flying through the air and the soft *thud* when they hit the target. When the range came into view, Wishbone saw five boys and girls shooting arrows at the distant circular targets. A large wall, made of square bales of hay, stood behind the targets. Wishbone saw Rebecca working with one of the young girls. She placed the young girl's hands on the bow and its string.

Wishbone gave another sniff, looked around, then proceeded back down the trail the way he had come. *Everything checked out at the archery range,* Wishbone thought. The terrier didn't think he would spend much of his free time at the archery range. *Besides, who ever heard of a dog shooting a bow and arrow?*

The last stop on Wishbone's rounds was the basketball court. It was also located in a clearing surrounded by giant pine trees. The dog watched as Joe and the kids practiced passing the ball to one another. The drill was one Wishbone recognized. He had seen Joe do it many times during the boy's own basketball practice at home in Oakdale.

As Wishbone jumped up into the wooden bleachers next to the court, that strange feeling came over him again. Before breakfast that day, and in the camp's parking lot the day before, Wishbone had the creepy feeling of being watched. Both times it had happened, the terrier tried to get a whiff of some unseen intruder. Each time, however, he smelled nothing unusual.

Wishbone turned and looked into the surrounding trees. Just like the other times when he felt he was being watched, Wishbone didn't see anything. He tried to tell himself that his guard-dog sensitivity meter was set too high. There actually could have been plenty of different kinds of animals watching him from the thick woods. If they did, he probably wouldn't be able to see them either. But his instincts told him that it was not an animal watching him. It felt like something else.

Joe had the kids run one more practice drill, but he could tell they were itching to play a real game. Joe introduced one of the drills his coach had used on his team. Joe had the ten nine-year-old boys stand in two rows directly across from each other. He threw one of the kids a basketball and had him pass it to the kid across from him. The boys would use the basic two-handed pass to move the ball down the line. When the ball was at the other end, the last one with the ball would pass it back to Joe. This seemed to be working great, except for one thing—Jack Conner.

"Heads up, Jack!" one of the campers said to the young boy. Jack held his hands up, ready to catch a pass. When the other boy quickly tossed the ball to Jack, his hands seemed to close too soon. The ball bounced off his hands and rolled off the court. The rest of the kids started to snicker.

"Come on, guys," Joe said to the group. Jack ran to get the ball. He had short brown hair and was a little smaller than the rest of the boys. To Joe, he seemed like a nice kid. He just wasn't very well coordinated.

"That's okay, Jack," Joe said, as the boy came back with the ball. He ran back and passed it to the player across from him. However, when the ball came back to him, he missed it again. The boy had similar problems with all the drills Joe had given the boys. Yet, he was still eager to play and to be a part of the group.

After a few more rounds, Joe stopped the drill. He randomly picked two kids to be team captains. As Joe watched the two boys choose teams, he realized he had made a mistake. Neither one of them was choosing Jack to be on their team. Joe knew it was too late to stop it, though. Soon there were only four kids left, then three, and then two. Then, what Joe realized would happen did happen. Jack was the last one picked.

Joe wanted to kick himself. He should have made up the teams himself. He hoped being picked last didn't further damage the young boy's confidence. Joe's own confidence about being a camp counselor was already shaky. Now, Joe was starting to doubt his coaching skills.

Once the teams were assembled, Joe started the game. Everyone played great. Well . . . almost everyone. Jack tried hard. The boy ran with great enthusiasm. Jack stayed right with the player he was supposed to cover when his team was on defense. When they were on offense, however, no one would pass him the ball, even when he was completely open.

Joe had seen it all before. There was always one kid who really wanted to play but just wasn't very good. Joe always sympathized with those kids. If Joe's father hadn't been a basketball coach when he was alive, and worked with him, Joe might have *been* one of those kids.

When Joe was twelve, he had temporarily coached girls' T-ball. Joe learned that coaching was not as easy as it looked. It took a good knowledge of the game, good communication skills, and patience— lots of patience. Now, Joe wasn't coaching T-ball. He was coaching basketball. That was his game. That was also his father's game. Joe didn't know if he would be as good a coach as his father had been. But he was going to try.

When the game was over and the campers were returning to their cabins to clean up, Joe held Jack back. Wishbone jumped down from the bleachers and joined him.

"Say, Jack," Joe said, "could you help me put away the equipment?"

"Sure," the young boy replied eagerly. Joe saw Wishbone approaching.

"How's it going, boy?" Joe asked, as he knelt to give the dog a pat.

Wishbone wagged his tail at the sound of Joe's voice.

Jack picked up a basketball, then seemed to give in to the urge to pet Wishbone. Joe noticed a lot of the campers had that urge. Joe also noticed that Wishbone didn't seem to mind it one bit.

The two boys patted Wishbone in silence. Then Joe finally said, "You know, you showed a little improvement out there."

"Are you sure you're talking about me?" Jack said with a puzzled look on his face.

"Yes, I'm talking about you," Joe said with a laugh. "You seem to really like the game."

"I do," Jack replied. "I just wish I was better at it."
He stopped petting Wishbone and just stared at the
basketball in his hands.

"You know," Joe said, "coordination and skill can
be improved with practice. But I don't think that's your
main problem."

The young boy looked up from the basketball.
"Then what is?" he asked.

"I think you lack self-confidence," Joe replied.
"Lack of self-confidence can throw any player's game
off." Joe stood and motioned for Jack to do the same.
"I want to teach you a trick my father taught me."
Jack stood, and Joe took the basketball out of the
boy's hands. "Now," Joe said, "I want you to close
your eyes and put your hands out, like you're going to
catch a pass."

"You're not going to throw me the ball with my
eyes closed, are you?" Jack asked. "I can't even catch it
when my eyes are open!"

"I wouldn't pass you a ball with your eyes closed,"
Joe said with a chuckle. "Just trust me."

The boy did as Joe said. He closed his eyes and put
his hands out in front of him, as if he were about to
catch a pass.

"Now," Joe began, "I want you to *visualize* me
throwing you a pass. And, more important, I want you
to visualize *catching* it."

"Okay," Jack agreed. His voice had a touch of
confused shakiness to it.

"Now, when I say 'go,' I want you to visualize the
pass," Joe instructed. "Are you ready?"

"I guess so," the boy answered.

"Okay," Joe said slowly, as if verbally winding up for a pitch. "And . . . *go!*"

Jack's hands came together, as if catching an invisible basketball. He smiled and opened his eyes.

"Don't open your eyes yet," Joe said. "Let's do it a few more times. Remember, visualize the pass, just as if it were real."

Joe had Jack catch the invisible ball about fifteen more times. Each time, Joe said the word *go!* a bit faster and closer to the last time he'd said it. Near the end of the exercise, Joe simply repeated the word with just a couple of seconds between each time.

"Now," Joe said calmly, "open your eyes."

Jack slowly opened his eyes. Then he widened them as Joe gently but quickly passed the basketball to him. Jack caught the ball without any hesitation or fumbling. Wishbone barked with approval.

"You see," Joe said with a smile. "*That* is what you are capable of. Your lack of self-confidence interferes with your abilities."

The young boy looked at the basketball in his hands. A look of amazement was in his eyes. Joe took the ball from Jack again and walked over to the nearby storage shed. He placed the ball into the shed, then closed the door, locking it with a padlock.

Joe joined Jack and Wishbone. Then, all together, they walked up the trail toward the main road. "I want you to practice some more passes," Joe said to the young boy. "But practice them in your mind. I know you can catch them. You just have to *visualize* yourself catching them."

Joe, Jack, and Wishbone came to the end of the

trail. They took a left onto the camp's main road and walked toward the cafeteria pavilion.

Jack broke the silence. "Do you really think that will help me get better at basketball?" the young boy asked.

"Sure," Joe replied. "As long as you do some real practicing, as well." They walked a bit farther. Joe heard the clicking from Wishbone's nails as he walked down the paved road. He looked down at the dog for a moment. Then Joe turned back to Jack. "Visualization really helped my free-throws," Joe said. "You would be surprised at what it can do."

Jack seemed to be in much better spirits than he had been when the basketball game had just ended.

Joe felt good about that. "Visualize whenever you get a chance," Joe continued. "When your game improves on the real court, your confidence will improve as well."

"Thanks, Joe," Jack replied, as they came to the trail that led to Jack's cabin. The young boy turned left and stepped onto the pine-needle-covered ground. Joe noticed a slight spring in Jack's step that hadn't been there before. That gave Joe a good feeling. He thought his father would be proud of him.

Wishbone's stomach told him it was getting close to lunchtime. As he and Joe headed for the cafeteria pavilion, Wishbone trotted ahead, investigating the campgrounds. The dog sniffed out the entire area. He passed the trail leading south, toward the pool. Just after that, there was a small hill the main road climbed before it led to the cafeteria. Wishbone trotted to the top of the hill, his nose still pointed at the ground.

His nose quickly came across a half-empty hot-dog bun plastic bag.

"What's this doing here?" the dog asked.

He looked up. From his position at the top of the road's small hill, he could see the back of the cafeteria and the trails leading down to the docks and the bridge. He saw plastic bread bags and pieces of bread thrown all around the side of the road and near the back of the cafeteria.

"Hey! This just isn't right!"

The dog darted down the hill and scooped up an empty bag in his mouth and carried it back over the hill. The terrier walked right up to Joe, looked up at him, then dropped the bag on the ground.

"Joe!" he said. "This spells trouble!"

Joe leaned down and picked up the empty bag. "Where did you get this, Wishbone?" Joe asked, looking at the bag.

"Come on!" Wishbone barked. "Our food supply needs us!" He ran back up the hill. The dog could hear the sound of running behind him.

When they had made their way over the hill, Wishbone looked back and saw Joe picking up empty plastic bags. As Wishbone and Joe made their way back toward the cafeteria, Wishbone soon saw Barry doing the same thing. The senior counselor had a trash bag and was filling it full of bread scraps and half-empty bread bags. Three of the campers, two young girls and a young boy, were helping out, as well.

"What happened?" Joe asked, as he walked toward Barry. The senior camp counselor held open the trash bag. Joe dumped his handful of plastic bags into it.

"Sometimes the animals get into the storage lockers," Barry replied. He bent down and picked up the bag that Wishbone was offering him.

"Hey!" Wishbone said. "I'm the only animal that should be allowed in those lockers!"

Wishbone watched as the three young campers approached and offered what they had picked up. Each of them, in turn, dumped their trash into Barry's open bag.

Barry looked around the area. "That looks like everything," he said with a smile. "Thanks, kids." The three campers said their good-byes and left.

Barry, Joe, and Wishbone turned toward the two storage lockers. Wishbone noticed that neither locker had windows of any kind. He also noticed the locked padlocks on both locker doors. He wondered how animals could have broken in.

"How did the animals get inside the lockers?" Joe asked Barry.

Barry set down the full garbage bag and reached into his pocket. Wishbone heard the jingling of keys as the older counselor pulled out a key chain filled with keys. Wishbone thought the teenager must have had a key to every lock in camp on that key chain. Barry found the right key and inserted it in one of the padlocks. He looked puzzled. Barry seemed to be taking a long time to answer Joe's question.

Finally, Barry spoke. "It was locked. I don't under-

stand how anyone could have gotten inside," he replied. He checked the second padlock. It was also locked.

Wishbone looked at the heavy latches that held the doors shut even once the padlocks had been removed. Wishbone thought Barry would have had to leave the doors unlatched for the animals to get into the lockers. *Either that, or the raccoons around here have been working out at the gym,* the dog thought.

"I didn't see the plastic bags on my way to breakfast," Joe remarked. "Are you sure it happened last night?"

"Look, Joe," Barry said impatiently, "I'm really busy. I have to get ready for lunch." The senior counselor stepped into one of the lockers.

"Can I help out in some way?" Joe asked, stepping up to the locker's open doorway.

"Me, too!" Wishbone said. "I'm always willing to help when it comes to food!" The terrier poked his head into the open doorway to get a peek. He saw the senior counselor looking up at one of the many shelves full of food.

"No, that's okay, Joe," Barry said, pulling a large cardboard box off one of the shelves. "It's Jeremy's turn to help out in the kitchen. He should be here soon." Barry carried the large box toward the locker door. Joe and Wishbone stepped back to let him pass. "Take some time off," Barry added. He shut the locker door with one hand.

Wishbone watched Barry carry the box toward a kitchen counter. He wondered why Barry had been short-tempered with Joe. He also seemed jittery. Maybe he felt badly for leaving the locker doors unlocked. Something else also bothered Wishbone. He knew that if the animals had gotten into the food locker last night, he would have seen the mess early that morning, when he had made his rounds. In fact, Barry himself would have seen it when he was preparing breakfast. Wishbone thought the mess had to have been made sometime later that morning.

"Come on, Wishbone," Joe said. "Let's see how David is doing." Together, the two hiked toward the swimming pool.

Wishbone was kind of embarrassed. After all, it was his first day as head of summer camp security, and some prank had already occurred right under his usually highly alert nose. He didn't like that one bit. The dog would double his detecting efforts. He would double his rounds! He would double his meals!

Well, for all of that extra work, he would need double the strength.

Two eyes peered through the underbrush and carefully watched the dog and the boy. The two walked away from the storage lockers and headed toward the main road.

Chapter Five

That night, at dinner, it was Joe's turn to help Barry in the cafeteria. Joe helped the senior counselor serve dinner and clean up after everyone was finished eating. Wishbone really seemed to enjoy Joe's temporary assignment. The terrier seemed more than happy to sample any dish that Barry had prepared. Joe also noticed that Barry seemed a bit more at ease when Wishbone was around.

After almost everything in the cafeteria had been cleaned and put away, Barry told Joe he could leave if he wanted to. All Barry had left to do was plan the next day's breakfast, and he didn't need Joe for that. Joe said good-night to Barry, and he and Wishbone left the cafeteria.

They walked out from under the brightly lit pavilion. When they stepped onto the trail leading to the main road, Joe turned on his flashlight. He looked up toward the sky. The quarter moon gave off very little light. With the light shining from the cafeteria combined with the lampposts that lined the main road, Joe could see well enough without using his flashlight. Joe turned it on, anyway, just to be sure he and Wishbone could make their way safely.

Joe and Wishbone soon stepped onto the hard asphalt of the main road. They were about to turn left, toward the cabins, when Joe spotted something out of the corner of his eye. He turned, glancing toward the safety tower and then toward the inlet bridge. In the distance, toward the bridge, he saw a bright, flickering speck. He squinted his eyes and, after peering a little longer, Joe thought it looked like a distant campfire. It was burning near the part of the camp that was closed.

Joe started to walk back to the cafeteria to get Barry. Then, suddenly, he stopped. Joe thought the campfire might have been built by some of the young campers. Maybe a few of them had decided to sneak off and have a little adventure.

Joe turned back to the main road and started to walk toward the campfire. Wishbone trotted alongside him. Part of the responsibility of being a camp counselor was to round up stray campers. He was also concerned about an unauthorized campfire. Joe thought it was nothing he couldn't handle by himself— well, himself and Wishbone, anyway.

The two walked down the unused trail, heading toward the bridge. The trail was much narrower than the others. The trees and bushes seemed to reach out for Joe as he went by. The trail was also very dark. The row of lampposts on the main road didn't extend down that particular trail. The only light came from the flashlight Joe aimed at the ground. With the black forest around him, sometimes it felt as if he and Wishbone were traveling through a dark tunnel.

When they reached the end of the trail, Joe and Wishbone found themselves right next to the lake. The faint moonlight cast an eerie, colorless light over the long, thin wooden bridge stretched out before them. The bridge crossed the lake's large indentation that cut deeply into the land. Joe looked toward the other side and still saw the flickering light of what seemed to be an unauthorized campfire. The opposite bank of the lake looked as if it were about fifty yards away, but the fire seemed to be burning further away, deep in the woods. The thick growth of trees kept Joe from seeing anyone who might be around the fire. He thought he would find out who was there soon enough.

Joe took one cautious step onto the old bridge. Jeremy and Rebecca had said the bridge was unsafe. To be extra careful, Joe stayed to one side, where he thought the boards would be strongest. He tested each step lightly before he put his entire weight on a certain spot. He held onto the two wooden handrails that lined each side of the bridge. Joe did not place too much faith in them, though. He put his hands on them only to keep his balance. He was not going to take any chances.

Joe turned back to check on Wishbone. He saw that the dog was right behind him, following him with confidence. Joe would rather have kept Wishbone off the bridge completely, but his pal was crossing the bridge with no difficulty. Besides, the terrier didn't weigh nearly as much as Joe. If the old bridge could

support Joe's weight, it certainly would support Wishbone's.

The bridge was missing boards in some places, the handrails wobbled, and the wooden planks creaked with each step Joe took. Still, he made it across confidently. Once he had made it to the other side, he saw a trail that led up a small hill toward the cabins. Joe and Wishbone walked up the hill. The firelight bounced off the trees.

When boy and dog got to the top of the hill, Joe saw the small campfire burning. The firelight created a clear circle of light. It lit up the closest trees and cabins. Joe looked around. There was no one else there. He shone his flashlight into the woods.

"You can come out now," Joe said in a firm, loud voice. He assumed the campers had run off into the woods when they heard or saw Joe and Wishbone crossing the bridge. "You're not in any trouble," he added. "I just want to talk to you."

Joe continued to scan the woods for any sign of mischievous campers. Wishbone took a couple of steps closer to the fire. Joe watched as the dog's attention strayed from the fire to something sitting close by.

Joe moved his flashlight beam to fall upon whatever Wishbone had found. When the light hit the object, Joe took a couple of steps closer to it. He saw that Wishbone was looking at a tomahawk, sticking out of a log. It looked as if someone had tried to split the log in two and then had left the tomahawk there.

Joe stepped forward slowly. He bent over and reached out toward the ancient-looking weapon. It was probably authentic and Native American. Just as his fingertips were inches away from the tomahawk's handle, he heard the sound of a slow-beating drum coming from the woods.

Immediately, Joe whirled around and aimed his flashlight at the source of the noise. The bright beam pointed to where the sound came from, but Joe saw only trees. His heart began to race as his eyes darted from tree to tree, trying to find the source of the drumbeats.

Suddenly, a second pounding of drumbeats came from the woods behind him. Joe turned around quickly. He turned the flashlight toward the second set of sounds. Still he saw nothing. The drums were beating faster and faster. Wishbone barked as Joe pointed the flashlight in front of him, then behind him. Joe's heart was beating faster with every second that passed.

"Who's there?" Joe asked nervously.

Joe's pulse raced, and beads of sweat began to form on his forehead. The drumbeats were coming even faster. Joe's heart seemed to be pounding in time with the rapid beats.

"Who is it?" Joe asked again, his voice even more shaky than before. He immediately looked for Wishbone to make sure the dog was nearby. After locating Wishbone, Joe scanned the forest. He hoped his light would land on whoever was beating the drums. *What if there is no one?* Joe thought. *What if the drums aren't real drums?* Joe's heart felt as if it would burst out of his chest. *What if it's the ghost of Ka Nowa——*

WHOOOOSH!!!

Joe leaped back as the tiny campfire suddenly exploded. A large blue flame shot high up into the air.

That was all Joe needed to push him into action. Joe knew he had to get back to the main part of the camp immediately and tell the other counselors what had just happened. Followed closely by Wishbone, Joe quickly made his way down the trail and headed for the bridge. This time, Joe and Wishbone didn't cross the bridge as slowly or carefully as they had on the way over. They had an urgent mission now.

"Hey!" Wishbone said, as everyone stepped into the abandoned campsite. Joe, David, Sam, and Barry were all shining their flashlights around the area.

"Where did it go?" Joe said, his voice sounding confused. He stepped toward the spot where the fire had been. "It was all right here—the fire, the log with the tomahawk in it . . . everything." The counselors shone lights on the spots Joe indicated. There was nothing there.

"Are you *sure* this was where everything was?" David asked.

"Could the fire have been over by some of the other cabins?" Barry added.

Joe seemed confused. "No. I'm telling you, it was right here," he said, looking frustrated. "It was right by these cabins, on *this* side of the bridge."

"We believe you, Joe," Sam said. "It's just not here now."

Wishbone was confused, as well. It had taken him and Joe only about ten minutes to go round up the others. Now they were in the exact place they were before, yet there was no fire, no drumbeat, no tomahawk—nothing. Then, again, how much time did a ghost need to make everything disappear? Wishbone didn't think a ghost needed much.

"Don't worry, Joe," Barry said. "A dark camp, an abandoned campsite, and a ghost story can play tricks on anyone's mind." The senior counselor turned and began to walk toward the bridge. "Don't let it get to you," he added. Barry disappeared down the trail.

"I don't believe it," Joe said to himself. "He thinks I'm imagining everything."

"Don't worry, Joe," David reassured his friend. "I'm sure we'll figure out what's going on."

Wishbone noticed that David sounded doubtful about what he was saying. Then, suddenly, Wishbone heard another noise. It was coming from the bridge. Was it more drums?

Everyone looked toward the trail as two flashlight beams danced through the trees. Soon, Jeremy and Rebecca appeared. Wishbone relaxed. *That's good,* Wishbone thought. *No ghost there.*

"We heard you saw a fire or something over here," Jeremy said excitedly.

"Was it the ghost?" Rebecca asked.

"There's no such thing as ghosts," David said.

Wishbone didn't think David sounded totally convinced himself.

"I don't know what it was," Joe said, a bit embarrassed and confused.

Wishbone didn't like to see his best friend upset like this. He trotted over to Joe and placed his muzzle against the boy's leg.

"You saw it, didn't you, boy?" Joe said quietly, as he scratched Wishbone behind the ears.

"That's right, Joe," Wishbone replied, his tail wagging. The dog started to sniff around the ground. "And I'm going to find out what's going on—or I'll hand in my guard-dog license."

Wishbone began to give the abandoned campsite area a thorough sniffing. If it was a ghost and it left a scent trail, Wishbone was determined to find it. His nose locked onto a strong, and strangely appealing, scent. The Jack Russell terrier followed the strong smell to its source. It was coming from Jeremy's and Rebecca's shoes.

"Hey! Where did you get that mud?" Wishbone asked, barking at the brother and sister as he circled around their feet. A bright flashlight beam fell on the little dog.

"What's wrong, Wishbone?" Sam asked. Her flashlight beam moved from the dog to the two counselors' feet. "What's on your shoes?"

Jeremy and Rebecca both pointed their flash-

lights toward their own feet. "Oh, that's just mud," Rebecca replied.

"Yeah. We've been working down by the canoes," Jeremy added.

"That's some great-smelling stuff," Wishbone said. The mud around the lake smelled a lot different from the mud back in Oakdale. The lake mud was full of all sorts of algae and fungus that really added a special aroma to its general odor. Wishbone thought it was a great smell. Unfortunately, it was also a very strong smell. In fact, it was so strong that it made the act of tracking down any lingering ghost smells almost impossible. *That is too bad,* Wishbone thought. *I really wanted to find out what a ghost smells like—from a distance, of course.*

"Well, there's definitely nothing here now," Sam said to Joe. "Maybe we should come back and investigate in the daylight." She seemed as if she were trying to cheer Joe up. "I bet we will find a trace of something then."

"I guess so," Joe said.

Wishbone knew that Joe had seen something because he had also, even if everyone else didn't believe him. The terrier put his nose to the ground once more. Mud smell or no mud smell, Wishbone had to find a trace of something.

As everyone else started to walk back to the bridge, Wishbone sniffed his way over to the spot where he and Joe had seen the fire. The air was still thick with the mud smell, but Wishbone found something of interest.

As the dog placed his nose near the spot where the

fire had been, he felt warmth. He sniffed around some more. There was a clue, after all. Wishbone found an actual circle of warm ground. The circle was about the same size as the ghostly campfire had been. *Wait a minute,* Wishbone thought. *If the campfire wasn't real, then why is this spot of ground still warm?*

The dog turned to give a bark to the others. Unfortunately, they had already reached the bridge. A few circles of light from the kids' flashlights danced through the distant trees and then disappeared. Wishbone was completely alone. In the dark.

"You know," Wishbone said with a bark, "maybe it *would* be a good idea to come back here in the daylight. Hey, guys!" The dog tore down the trail to join the others.

Chapter Six

The next morning, it was Sam's turn to help Barry in the cafeteria. Wearing long white aprons, she and Barry stood behind the serving counter and dished out breakfast to the line of campers. Sam dipped her long metal serving spoon into a heated tray of scrambled eggs. She lifted a heaping spoonful of the fluffy eggs and placed a serving on each camper's plastic tray. Even Wishbone came by for a tidbit after he had finished his dog food. Camp food was quickly becoming one of his favorite after-meal snacks.

When all the campers had gotten their breakfast and sat down to eat, Sam and Barry each put together a tray of food and joined the others. Normally, the counselors would have split up so that each one would sit with a small group of campers. That morning, however, the six counselors and Mr. Alexander sat together at one of the large wooden picnic tables. Sam had a pretty good idea of why they were all together.

"When several of us returned to the abandoned

campsite last night," Joe was explaining to the group at his table, "there wasn't a trace of anything I'd seen before, when just Wishbone and I were there."

Sam sat on the side of the table where David and Joe were. Barry sat on the other side with Rebecca and Jeremy. Mr. Alexander was sitting in a chair at the head of the table.

Sam listened as Joe finished the story about what had happened the night before. As she ate her breakfast slowly, she noticed Joe had hardly touched his food. He still must have been upset about the previous evening.

"We were going to go over there today—in broad daylight," David added. "Maybe we can find a clue then."

"I don't think that's such a good idea," Mr. Alexander answered after taking a sip of coffee. Steam rose from his warm mug and disappeared into the cool morning air. "That bridge isn't safe at all. The last thing I want is for someone to get hurt while investigating these events."

These *events*? Sam thought. *What does that mean?*

"Kids," the camp owner said after another sip of coffee, "this isn't the first time something like this has happened." He set his mug down on the wooden table. "I really should have told you sooner. I just didn't want to scare you."

"What *else* has happened?" Joe asked suspiciously.

"Well . . ." Mr. Alexander said, and he took in a deep breath. He gave a look to Barry, Jeremy, and Rebecca. "It all started harmlessly enough, I guess. The first couple of weeks after we opened the camp, when we were fixing up the place, things started to get arranged strangely. Once, I found that the tables and benches here in the cafeteria had all been stacked into a giant pyramid."

Rebecca jumped in. "All the arrows from the archery range were crammed into every one of the bull's-eyes of every one of the targets."

Next, Jeremy spoke. "We saw other campfires burning deep in the woods. But when we made our way to where we thought they were, the fires had vanished."

"That was back when all the strange events were still harmless," Mr. Alexander said. "Recently, the pranks have become more destructive." He gestured to the red-haired boy. "Jeremy is constantly repairing canoes that get mysteriously damaged. They keep getting slashes cut into them—possibly with a hatchet."

"Or a tomahawk?" Joe asked.

"I suppose it could have been," Mr. Alexander responded.

"What else has happened?" David asked.

"Well," the man continued, "someone kept loosening the boards on the footbridge. It's happened so much that we finally gave up repairing it. I'm surprised none of you kids fell when you crossed that rickety thing."

"That's what you meant on the first day," Sam said, turning to Jeremy. "You said the old bridge *used* to be safe."

Mr. Alexander spoke. "I told them not to say anything about the incidents," he said. "As I said, I didn't want to frighten you away. I see now that I should have told you and your parents. This was irresponsible of me. But I truly did not think anyone would be harmed. I'm having my doubts, now." The camp owner motioned to Wishbone. "That is actually why I wanted Wishbone to stay." The dog looked up at Mr. Alexander and wagged his tail. Mr. Alexander continued. "I thought having a dog around might scare off the pranksters."

"Don't forget to tell him about the food," Barry chimed in.

"And there's the food-storage lockers," Mr. Alexander said, shaking his head. "Someone keeps getting into them and scattering the food everywhere."

Sam noticed that Wishbone seemed to be taking a special interest in that part of the mystery. The dog walked over to Barry's side of the table and wagged his tail.

"We used to think animals were finding a way to break into them somehow," Barry said. "The food would be everywhere, and yet the doors would still be locked." He looked around the table. "We just couldn't figure out how it was happening. And now, since it's starting to occur during the daytime, I don't think it's animals."

"That's what happened yesterday?" Joe asked.

Barry nodded his head, and Mr. Alexander gave a look around the table. "Again, I'm sorry I didn't tell you kids and your parents about this before you signed on," Mr. Alexander said. "If you want to leave, I will certainly understand."

Sam looked around the table. She didn't want to

leave. She looked at David and Joe. Joe didn't look as confident as David did, but she didn't think Joe wanted to leave, either.

"I don't want to leave," David announced. "And I don't believe in ghosts, so there must be a logical explanation for all of those events."

"I agree," Sam said. "I bet we can find out who's doing these things."

Mr. Alexander turned to Joe. "What about you, Joe?"

Sam watched as Wishbone placed his two front paws onto the bench Joe was sitting on. "I'll stay," Joe said, as he gave the dog a scratch behind the ears. "But if I see another ghost campfire, I'm rounding you all up *before* I investigate."

Everyone laughed.

The group continued to eat their breakfast. Sam ate a little faster than normal. She still had to help Barry with the cleanup, then get over to her horseback-riding class.

"It sounds as if someone is trying to get Camp Ka Nowato to shut down," David said between mouthfuls of food. "Do you have any idea who would want to do that, Mr. Alexander?"

Mr. Alexander looked at Barry, then back to David. "Barry seems to think it's Blue Bear Inc."

"Who's Blue Bear Inc.?" Sam asked.

"Blue Bear is a large corporation that owns most of the property around the lake," Barry replied. "It has several resorts in operation already. I'm sure Blue Bear would love to make the camp another one of its properties."

92

"Blue Bear did make me an offer on the camp," Mr. Alexander told the kids. "It was for a lot more money than I paid for it, but I still wanted to give camp life a go."

"You think someone from Blue Bear might be pulling these pranks in order to force you to sell?" Joe asked.

"I suppose it's a possibility," Mr. Alexander replied. "I just can't see a huge and respectable company like Blue Bear committing unlawful acts."

"Well, that's one suspect," David said quickly. "Who else could it be?"

"I really don't know," Mr. Alexander admitted.

"What about the previous owner of the camp?" Sam asked.

"Terrence Wells?" Mr. Alexander said, a look of surprise showing on his face. "Why would he want to shut down the camp?"

"You told me and my dad you got a really good deal on the camp," Sam replied. "What if he was angry about having to sell the camp so cheaply?"

Mr. Alexander thought for a moment. Then he spoke. "I don't know . . . maybe. I just assumed he wanted to get rid of it." Mr. Alexander took another sip from his coffee mug. "You see, Mr. Wells owned the camp for many years—when the camp was in its heyday." He set the mug down, then continued. "But then the camp ended up in a state of neglect like this. Maybe somewhere along the way, Mr. Wells stopped caring."

"Well, why didn't he sell the camp to Blue Bear?" David asked.

"Maybe the company didn't approach him," Mr. Alexander replied. "I didn't know about Blue Bear's interest in Camp Ka Nowato until after I had already bought it."

Sam took another bite of her eggs. It seemed as if they had quite a mystery to solve.

Wishbone left the conversation for a moment to make his rounds in the cafeteria. They weren't his official guard-dog rounds. They were his official hungry-dog rounds! When Barry had gone into town for supplies, he had bought Wishbone a healthy week's supply of dog food. Wishbone had already eaten his dog-food breakfast. However, after a bit of mingling with the campers . . . a piece of toast here . . . a bit of sausage there . . . Wishbone enjoyed an early-morning, after-breakfast snack. Besides, there was a mystery afoot! Wishbone could always think more clearly on a full stomach.

He made his way back to the counselors' table. It appeared they were still making a list of suspects.

"If you ask me," Jeremy said, after swallowing a piece of toast, "it's the people from Flaming Arrow."

"Flaming Arrow?" Sam asked. "Who's that?"

"Camp Flaming Arrow," Rebecca explained. "That's the name of the summer camp across the lake."

"Mr. Alexander," Jeremy said, "remember when we were cleaning out the office? We found those boxes full of trophies and photographs from some sort of inter-camp competition."

"Oh, right," Mr. Alexander said with a smile. "I forgot all about those."

Rebecca said to Sam and the others, "From the look of all that stuff, it seemed that Camp Ka Nowato and Camp Flaming Arrow were rivals for quite some time."

"So maybe some people from Flaming Arrow have been sneaking over here and pulling pranks," Sam said. "Maybe they're trying to start up the old rivalry."

"Maybe," Mr. Alexander said thoughtfully. "One thing is for sure. We don't have enough attendance or staff here to set up any new inter-camp competitions yet." The man drank the last of his coffee. "I am not even getting to fully enjoy my first week of summer camp. I have been stuck in my office working on getting more staff and campers for the rest of the summer."

"Any luck?" Sam asked.

"Some," Mr. Alexander replied. "I have been working so hard, I bet the phone lines and the Internet are still smoking from yesterday."

"You have access to the Internet?" David asked excitedly.

"The camp may look a bit old-fashioned," Mr. Alexander said, "but I'm not."

From the expression on David's face, Wishbone could tell he had gotten an idea.

"Could I use your computer to do some on-line investigating?" David asked Mr. Alexander. "Maybe I can find out a little bit more about Blue Bear Inc."

"I don't see why not, David," Mr. Alexander replied. "In fact, it would give me an excuse to get out

of the office for a while." He turned to the others. "You know, I didn't buy this camp just to stay cooped up indoors all day."

The kids laughed.

As everyone finished breakfast, Wishbone stepped out from under the shelter of the cafeteria's overhang and trotted under the green branches of the surrounding trees. The dog peered into the thick woods. He would have to be on extra-high alert now. Someone was pulling pranks around camp, and as the official camp guard dog, he would have to put a stop to the events. He would be the best guard dog he could be. Wishbone vowed to make the original camp guard dog proud—the spirit of Native American Ka Nowato.

Wishbone was about to return to the outdoor cafeteria when some thoughts entered his mind. *What if there isn't an outside prankster? What if the ghost of Ka Nowato is the one really playing the pranks? What if the ghost is trying to run everyone off of the Chitowa people's sacred burial ground?*

How could Wishbone guard against the original guard dog himself? Wishbone stepped back into the cafeteria. The terrier wondered how he could possibly guard against a ghost.

After breakfast, Sam and Barry washed the trays, utensils, and cooking gear. Since her father had bought Pepper Pete's, Sam had gained lots of experience washing up in a kitchen. She looked at the towering treetops just beyond the pavilion. Cleaning up in an outdoor sink, however, was something different.

As Sam scrubbed another plastic tray, she let her mind wander. She thought about everything she and the others had discussed so far that morning. Sam supposed any one of the three suspects they had talked about could have the motive to do such a thing. However, she felt that a couple of the suspects' motives didn't need to resort to vandalism. All in all, a strange turn of events had taken place in their summer camp experience.

As Sam scrubbed the last remaining tray, her mind wandered again. This time it took her back to Agatha Christie's *A Caribbean Mystery*. She thought about the part of the story she had read the night before.

At the Golden Palm Hotel, Miss Marple had discovered a disturbing turn of events, as well. Early one morning, Major Palgrave, the elderly gentleman with the glass eye and the fondness for telling stories, was found dead in his room. The hotel doctor ruled that Major Palgrave's death was a result of natural causes. It appeared he had a heart attack. In fact, the doctor found high-blood-pressure medication in Major Palgrave's room.

Miss Marple, however, wasn't so sure. After all, just the day before, Major Palgrave had been talking about a murder. Miss Marple recalled how the major was just about to show her a photograph of the murderer. He had then seen something that made him quickly put it away in his wallet. Then he pretended to be talking about something else. Did he see *something* or *somebody*?

Miss Marple was now very curious about the photograph the major was going to show her. He had said it had been a photograph of the man who quite possibly murdered his wife. Miss Marple decided she would investigate the matter.

She asked the doctor if he could look through the major's belongings and see if he could find a photograph of a man. Miss Marple lied and told the doctor that she had let the major look at a photograph of her nephew. The major had then put it with his other photographs by mistake. Secretly, she hoped the doctor would return with the photo the major was going to show her—the photo of the murderer.

The doctor fell for Miss Marple's plan. Unfortunately, he returned from the major's room with nothing. He informed Miss Marple that no photograph of a man was found among Major Palgrave's personal items. Miss Marple thought that was very strange. It seemed as if the photograph had completely disappeared.

Sam could barely wait to read more of *A Caribbean Mystery* that night. Right at the moment, however, she realized she and the others had a mystery of their own to investigate. The missing photograph of the murderer would have to wait.

Chapter Seven

Wishbone trotted down the camp's main road, his guard-dog senses set on full alert. As he made his way past the trail that led to the camp's pool, he heard footsteps approaching. The dog turned to see six campers running up the trail.

Wishbone quickly leaped off to one side. "Who goes there?" the guard dog called in a voice of authority. He positioned himself in the middle of the road. When the young children saw Wishbone, they quickened their pace instead of halting.

"Coming from the pool, eh?" Wishbone said. "Okay, let's see some I.D.!"

As the group of young boys and girls approached, Wishbone noticed they were all carrying towels. The kids stopped and gathered around Wishbone.

Looking up at them, he said, "Everyone has a towel, I see." He noticed they were still a bit wet. "Well," Wishbone said, "it looks like your story checks out."

He wagged his tail as the young campers knelt to pet him.

As the kids scratched and stroked his fur, Wishbone said, "Okay, you can pet me—but just a little. I *am* on duty, you know." The campers stopped petting the terrier and continued on the main road.

Wishbone went in the direction of the camp office. Suddenly, a thought occurred to him. Actually, his stomach growled, and that led him to the occurring thought. Hadn't he decided that the food-storage lockers had been broken into during the daytime? The dog had already inspected them thoroughly after breakfast, but he thought maybe he should check them again before continuing his rounds. It definitely couldn't hurt. *Besides,* the dog thought, *from the sound of my stomach, it's past time for my late-morning, pre-lunch snack!*

Wishbone trotted in the opposite direction and headed toward the cafeteria. When he reached the cafeteria, he saw Mr. Alexander sitting on one of the tables. His feet rested on a nearby bench. Barry was standing next to him. They seemed to be in the middle of a serious discussion, so Wishbone decided not to bother them. His pre-lunch snack could wait—for the moment, anyway.

The terrier quickly turned his attention to the back of the cafeteria. Wishbone trotted around toward the area, near the edge of the woods. To his satisfaction, he found that both lockers were locked securely. After a couple of sniffs, he also noticed no unusual scents nearby . . . well, except for one.

That was the one smell, however, that he hadn't quite been able to identify. Wishbone had noticed that the odor was all over the camp. It wasn't like any human smell he had come across before. It wasn't like any animal smell he had sniffed out before, either. Sometimes it was really strong. Other times the smell was very weak, as if whatever had been leaving it had not been in that area for a very long time. He didn't know what the smell belonged to.

He found the unidentified scent on and near the food-storage lockers. Wishbone guessed that whoever or whatever the smell belonged to had not been by the lockers for at least twenty-four hours. Actually, that was about how long ago it was when the food-storage lockers had been broken into. Wishbone was putting his nose to the ground to take in another sample smell when a thought crossed his mind. *I wonder what a ghost smells like.*

Suddenly, Wishbone got that creepy feeling again, the strange feeling that something was watching him. He looked around. Wishbone tried to convince himself that the ghost story from the first night at camp had just stirred up his imagination. Then, again, Wishbone remembered having that "being watched" feeling *before* Mr. Alexander had even told everyone the ghost story. What if that feeling came over him because there really *was* a ghost of Ka Nowato? What if the ghost *was* watching him? Then, again, maybe it really *was* just his imagination.

All of a sudden, a rustling noise came from the nearby woods. The fur on Wishbone's back stood on end. He whipped his head around to see what had made the noise. He peered into the thick woods but saw nothing. He lifted his nose high in the air, but he couldn't catch the scent from whatever had made the sound. *What if it's the ghost?* the dog thought. *What if it has come back to break into the food lockers again?*

The dog crouched and slowly creeped toward the direction of the intruder's sound. *Whatever it is,* Wishbone thought, *I have to be brave.* The dog took another step toward the woods. *Ghost or no ghost, I am the camp's guard dog now!* A few more steps . . .

And, more important, Wishbone thought, as a growl began to sound deep in his throat, *I have to . . .*

He was almost at the edge of the forest.

. . . protect . . .

Ahead, a small bush shook.

. . . the food!

Wishbone jumped bravely up into the air. *"Hooooooowha-cha!"* He landed in front of the rustling bush and barked with all his strength. "Come out of there! I have you surrounded!" he said.

The bush exploded with a blur of feathers and the sound of flapping wings. A wild pheasant burst from behind the leaves.

"Whoa!" Wishbone jumped out of the way of the bird's large, fluttering wings.

Confused, the pheasant awkwardly hovered in front of Wishbone for a moment.

"Sorry," the dog said, "I thought you were someone else."

Seeing Wishbone, the frightened bird flew up and over the cafeteria. It quickly disappeared into the distance as it made its way into the trees on the other side of the pavilion.

Wishbone's heart raced from being startled by the bird. He was also relieved at the same time. It hadn't been the ghost. He looked all around him. No one seemed to have noticed his barking. The terrier raised his muzzle and drew in another deep breath. There weren't any other strange smells around.

"This area is secure," Wishbone announced in a confident, deep voice as he headed back to the main road. "Time to continue my rounds."

The guard dog trotted in the direction of the council ring. He felt good about having chased something out into the open, even if it had been only a bird. There had been a couple of pranks pulled right under his very nose. Since he hadn't done anything to stop those pranks, Wishbone felt as if he was letting Mr. Alexander down.

Since he had already checked out most of the camp before breakfast, Wishbone decided just to skip the council ring and go to the camp's parking lot. Once he was sure the parking lot was secure, he would move on to another area. He followed the main road until it opened up onto the camp's parking lot. Wishbone looked around, gave a few sniffs, then decided to check the camp buses parked on the other side of the parking lot, to his left.

As Wishbone approached the buses, he glanced over his left shoulder at the camp office. He suddenly went on alert. Wishbone noticed that the camp office door was slightly open. Normally, the open door would not have been anything unusual. When Mr. Alexander was working inside the camp office, he often left the door open a crack, or sometimes wide open. However, Wishbone had just seen Mr. Alexander at the cafeteria talking to Barry. The terrier hadn't been at camp long, but he had been there long enough to pick up a few of the camp's routines. One of those routines was that whenever Mr. Alexander would leave the office, he would lock the door behind him. Wishbone knew that someone other than Mr. Alexander had been in the office and forgot to lock the door. Or, someone was in the office now.

The guard dog immediately snapped into his high-alert mode. The hair on his back stood on end as he crept slowly toward the camp office. This was his chance to show Mr. Alexander he had made the right decision in making Wishbone the camp guard dog. The prankster *had* to be inside the small building. This time, Wishbone was going to catch whoever it was red-handed.

David placed a folded towel onto the wooden chair. He had just come from one of his swimming classes and hadn't had time to change into dry clothes. Although the summer sun had mostly dried his swimming trunks on the walk from the pool to the camp office, they were still a bit damp. David didn't want Mr. Alexander to come back to the camp office and sit in a wet seat.

The camp office was a little larger than the counselors' cabins. Since it was filled mostly with stacks of cardboard boxes, it did not seem very big. David saw an open doorway leading to a second room at the back of the office. Through the doorway, he saw a small bed similar to the ones in his cabin. That was where Mr. Alexander slept. Tall stacks of boxes were cleared aside so a narrow path led to the back-room. To David, it looked like one of the camp's narrow trails.

As David reentered the office area, he saw that the desk in front of him was covered with paperwork. A quick glance showed one of the stacks to be job applications. The rest of the desk space was taken up by the camp's computer system—a keyboard, mouse, and monitor. David noticed that the computer sat under the desk encased in a tall, beige case. David reached down to the floor and turned the computer on.

Then David reached for a black-plastic case that he had brought with him. He opened the case. Inside were several CDs. The small collection of disks was David's computer safety pack. He carried them with him almost everywhere he went. It contained several disks with reference material, and one disk with computer anti-virus and safety programs. He removed that disk and placed it into the computer's CD-ROM drive.

David knew a lot about computers. He used the anti-virus and safety programs to protect himself against hackers. A "hacker" was the name given to people who generally used their knowledge of computers against others. David never did that. He did, however, use safeguards. Once the computer was up and running, David began to install his special software. There were a few programs that would allow him to surf in cyberspace without anyone identifying who he was. To everyone else on the Internet, it would be as if he and the computer he was on were invisible.

Once all of David's software was running, he used the mouse to control the tiny arrow that sat on the computer's screen. David moved it until it rested over a tiny picture—icon—of a telephone. Under the telephone, the word *Internet* was printed. David clicked one of the buttons on the mouse and logged onto Camp Ka Nowato's Internet server. After a few moments, a Web-browsing program launched, and the screen was filled with the words *Welcome to Camp Ka Nowato*. Mr. Alexander had told him that the camp had its own Web site. The Web browser was automatically set to visit that site first. David made a mental note to visit Camp Ka Nowato's site later.

David typed in the address of a Web site he knew of that allowed people to search the Internet. The Internet-searching site came on to the screen. David did a search for Terrence Wells. A list of different people by that name came on to the screen. The list was quite long. David decided to try to narrow the search later.

David went back to the Web-searching site. This time he typed the words *Blue Bear*. The screen momentarily went blank. Then a list of Web sites flowed down the screen. There were several sites containing the word *blue* or the word *bear,* but only one contained both. David moved the mouse and clicked on the underlined phrase, *Blue Bear Inc.* After a few seconds, the introductory screen for the Blue Bear Inc. Web site appeared. A simple drawing of a large blue bear filled the screen almost completely. The bear snarled as one of its paws swiped at an enemy. David wondered if there were any bears in the woods surrounding Camp Ka Nowato.

Suddenly, the office door flew wide open as a loud growl filled the room. David turned quickly toward the door, half-expecting to see the blue-bear drawing come to life. Instead, David saw only a little white-with-brown-and-black-spots dog standing in the open doorway—Wishbone. Once it was clear that the dog recognized David, he stopped growling and gave his tail a couple of short wags. That was the second time the terrier had startled David since arriving at camp.

"Wishbone," David said, his heart still racing. "You've got to stop popping up like that!" The dog cocked his head to one side, as if in reply.

Wishbone took a few steps closer to David as the boy turned his attention back to the computer. Once again, David placed his hand on the computer's mouse. He moved it until the arrow was over the large blue bear. He clicked on the mouse button, and another page from the Blue Bear Web site appeared. This one seemed to be the site's introductory page. There were several large and colorful photographs of people playing tennis, riding horses, and swimming.

All their activities seemed to be taking place in a beautiful outdoor setting.

Scattered among the images, David saw several links, or places on the site, which, if he clicked on them, would bring up other pages. They listed such things as hotels, business opportunities, and contact information. One of those links read: *Stockholders' Area*. David moved the arrow over that type and clicked on the mouse. Instantly, a smaller window appeared and asked the viewer to enter a password.

David paused, his fingers hovering over the keyboard. Though David wasn't a hacker, he had read about some of the tricks they used. David knew that sometimes the Web masters—the people in charge of maintaining Web sites—would use common, easy-to-remember passwords. The passwords would come in especially handy if the Web master was in charge of several different sites at once.

Through David's experience on the Internet, he had come to know a few of the "common" passwords. He typed one in: *Master*. Instantly, another window appeared, telling him the password was incorrect. David deleted his former entry and typed in another one: *One*. Again, the same message appeared.

David stared at the waiting screen. Wishbone placed his front paws on the edge of David's seat. The boy looked down and gave the dog a couple of light pats on his head. Then he turned back to the computer and typed another password he knew: *Blaster*. There was a slight hesitation. Then the screen went blank. Then the words *Welcome, Stockholder* were posted across the top of the screen.

David certainly wasn't a stockholder, so he felt a bit guilty about being in that area. He planned just to take a quick look around and then exit from the system as fast as he could. After all, there was a chance Blue Bear had been the one pulling the pranks. And he was trying to protect the summer camp.

After the page had finished loading, David glanced over the various icons that would take him to a specific section of the stockholders' area. His eyes landed on one in particular—a tiny cartoon bulldozer. Under the bulldozer were the words *Future Developments*. He quickly clicked on the bulldozer, and the current screen disappeared and was replaced with a large map.

A note of familiarity struck in David's mind as he realized he was looking at a map of Blue Bear Lake and the surrounding area. Most of the lake's shoreline was sectioned off into individual portions. He saw a section on the northeast side of the lake that represented the nearby resort Mr. Alexander had spoken of at breakfast. A small bear symbol showed that it was the property of Blue Bear. Along the southeast side of the shore was a complex of condominium apartments.

On the north side of the lake, David saw a section labeled *Camp Flaming Arrow.* He followed the camp's property around to the west, where it ended. Next to the camp were several smaller areas that were sectioned off. David thought they might be private properties. To the south side of the lake, David saw the area representing Camp Ka Nowato. There was only one thing wrong. It wasn't labeled properly. Instead of the camp's name, the words *Future Pioneer Resort* were printed across the area.

For a moment, David thought he might be looking at a map of another lake. But then he recognized the small blue hand-shaped inlet that reached into Camp Ka Nowato's property. It was the same inlet the unsafe wooden bridge stretched across. That was definitely Camp Ka Nowato. And, from the look of things, Blue Bear had other plans for its future.

"Gotcha!" David said excitedly. He had to show this to Mr. Alexander and the other counselors. It didn't prove Blue Bear was definitely behind the pranks and ghostly episodes. It did prove, however, that the corporation had definite plans for the camp's property. David moved the mouse, and the arrow raced up the screen toward the tiny drawing of the computer printer. He planned to print out a copy of the Blue Bear map to show the others.

Just before David pressed the mouse, a bright yellow-and-black-striped window appeared in the middle of the screen. *Unauthorized Entry!* was flashing in bold, threatening letters. Although startled by the message's sudden appearance, David wasn't too worried. His safeguards were all up and running. He knew there was no way anyone could detect his computer's identity. His safety programs were the best. He felt completely safe.

Well, maybe not *completely* . . . Another message appeared on the screen. It took the place of the first one. It read: *Initiating Bear Trap.* David quickly decided that Mr. Alexander and the other counselors could take his word about the Blue Bear map. He tried to close the Web-browsing program. Nothing happened. Something was wrong.

But that seemed impossible. David's security software should have been protecting his identity. And, there shouldn't be any way the Web site could be blocking his commands. He was completely powerless. Although the idea seemed crazy, the boy wondered if perhaps the ghost of Ka Nowato was messing with the computer. He shook the thought from his mind. That was impossible. *Ghosts don't exist . . . do they?*

Another small window appeared on the screen. This one read: ***Confirming Intruder's Identity in 5 Seconds!*** David couldn't believe it. He tried to close the Web-browsing program again. Nothing. The message displayed the number *4*. It was counting down.

David tried to move the cursor so that he could click on the Internet connection itself. It would not move. ***Three seconds***. David stared at the warning message. He couldn't understand how a Web page could take control of his computer. He had no power to stop it. ***Two seconds. Power!***

That was it! David reached down toward the large case resting under the desk. His finger reached out for the power switch. ***One second***. David pushed the dark power switch on the computer. As he did so, he looked back to the monitor. He watched as the Web site disappeared. Only a black screen remained.

A chill shot up David's spine. When the computer's power was shut off, his link to the Internet was broken. But before the monitor had gone black, David saw something he didn't like. The type written inside Blue Bear's warning box had changed. The new type read: *Intruder identified . . . Hello, Camp Ka Nowato.*

David had been too late.

Chapter Eight

Wishbone and David ran down the main road toward the cafeteria. Wishbone's stomach told him it was almost lunchtime. Wishbone's intuition told him David had something to tell the other counselors. He sensed the boy's deep worry. Wishbone hoped David would feel better if he told the others what was on his mind. If that didn't work, maybe a nice lunch would help. That always did the trick for Wishbone.

As they got closer to the cafeteria, two other things told the dog it was lunchtime: First, Wishbone heard the lively conversation of the summer camp's residents gathered together in one place; second, the delicious, mouth-watering smell of grilled food floated through the air. Wishbone took in a deep sniff.

"Hot dogs!" Wishbone said with approval. "One of my favorite pick-me-ups!" At least they had become one of his favorites after he found out there actually wasn't any *dog* in them.

David and Wishbone both ran underneath the cafeteria's pavilion roof. All the campers were in a long line that stretched around the outside of the cafeteria. Hungry young campers passed in front of the serving station, where Barry and Mr. Alexander were dishing out lunch. Wishbone saw that all the other counselors were also standing in line. David quickly went over to Sam and motioned for Joe to join them.

Wishbone watched as David quietly told Sam and Joe what had happened to him while he was working on the computer.

"That's it!" Joe said. "Blue Bear must be pulling the pranks."

Wishbone felt a feeling of relief in Joe's voice. It was as if he was looking for someone to hold responsible for the strange events so he could rule out the camp's ghost.

"I wouldn't jump to conclusions, Joe," Sam said. "I think David's discovery only proves what Mr. Alexander has been saying all along."

"Yeah," David agreed. "It proves only that Blue Bear has an interest in the summer camp's property. We still don't have any proof that Blue Bear is behind the pranks."

Joe seemed disappointed. "Well," he began, "you have to admit that, at the very least, this puts Blue Bear at the top of the suspect list." Sam and David agreed, and Joe seemed more at ease. However, he didn't seem *completely* convinced that a ghost didn't exist.

"What do we do now?" Sam asked.

"I don't suppose there's really anything we *can*

do," David replied. "We just need to keep our eyes and ears open, and be especially alert."

"I've been doing that for the past few days," Wishbone said with a bark. The dog looked into the surrounding woods. "The second problem is, I think something out there is keeping its eyes and ears glued to us at the same time."

"I don't know," David added. "I still find it hard to believe a large corporation like Blue Bear would stoop to pulling the kind of serious pranks that have been going on." David glanced back at the long food line.

"I agree," Sam said, as she followed David's gaze. "But for now, I think we need to get back to the campers."

"Right," David agreed. "I'll tell Mr. Alexander what happened after we eat lunch."

"Lunch, what a great idea, David!" Wishbone said, as he wagged his tail. "I find that everything seems better when you have a full stomach."

The three kids made their way to the lunch line. Wishbone stood next to Joe. At first, Joe seemed to be comforted by what David had found out. But now, he seemed nervous again. Wishbone hoped the advice he had given David would work for Joe, as well. Maybe Joe would feel better after eating lunch.

And speaking of lunch! Wishbone couldn't wait to sample the delicious-smelling hot dogs that were being served at the other end of the line. The terrier lifted his nose high into the air. For the moment the hot dogs' tempting aroma would have to hold him over. Wishbone took in a deep breath. *Grilled, steamy hot dogs!*

*Freshly toasted buns! Relish! Mustard! Men's cologne . . .
Men's cologne?!!*

Wishbone looked around quickly to find the
source of the out-of-place scent. His gaze fell on two
men in dark suits. They were walking up the path
leading to the cafeteria. To Wishbone, the sight of the
two men in suits in a forest seemed out of place,
indeed. Their presence should be announced. He let
out a series of short, loud barks.

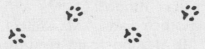

Joe heard Wishbone's barks and immediately
looked around. Two men in dark suits approached. The
one on the right was taller than the other, and he had
dark brown hair. The man on the left was shorter and
heavier. He, too, had short, dark brown hair. Both were
wearing dark sunglasses. Joe stepped away from the
lunch line and went to greet them.

"May I help you?" Joe asked.

"Hi, son. My name is Mr. French and my associate
is Mr. Miller. We're looking for Tom Alexander."

"Mr. French, Mr. Miller," said a voice from behind
Joe. The boy turned to see Mr. Alexander approaching. "I
haven't changed my mind, you know," the camp owner
said. "Or are you two just out for a stroll in the woods?"

"Well, we just wanted to make sure, Tom," Mr.
French said. Both of the men shook Mr. Alexander's
hand.

"We were down at one of our Blue Bear properties
across the lake," Mr. Miller began. "And we got a call
from the people who run the Blue Bear Web site."

Mr. French took up where Mr. Miller left off. "Apparently, you have been doing some research into our company."

A confused look came over Mr. Alexander's face. "I'm not sure what you mean," the camp owner said.

It was Mr. Miller's turn to speak. "Someone from Camp Ka Nowato was detected logging on to the Blue Bear Web site a little while ago."

"Actually, they were caught in our stockholders' area," Mr. French continued.

"That's a restricted area," Mr. Miller finished.

"What?" Mr. Alexander said. He turned to face the lunch line. "David," the man called.

Joe watched as David quickly came over to join the group. Mr. Alexander put a gentle hand on the boy's shoulder. "David," he said, "these men are from Blue Bear Incorporated. They say someone here accessed their Web site earlier. Do you know what they're talking about?"

David looked down, then faced the camp owner directly. "I'm sorry, Mr. Alexander. I was going to tell you after lunch."

Mr. Alexander turned to the two men. "I'm sorry, fellas," he said. "It looks like David, here, was surfing on the Web and oversurfed his boundaries."

"I'm sorry," David said to the two men. "I didn't mean . . ."

Mr. Miller interrupted him. "There's no harm done, kid."

"We just thought Mr. Alexander had possibly reconsidered our original offer to buy the camp," Mr. French finished.

"There is nothing top-secret in that file, anyway," Mr. Miller added.

"What about Blue Bear's plans to turn Camp Ka Nowato into a resort?" Joe said abruptly. The words were out of his mouth before he realized what he had said.

"And you are . . . ?" Mr. French asked. He gave Joe an annoyed look.

"This is Joe, one of our fearless counselors," Mr. Alexander said with a smile, trying to put an end to the tense atmosphere that had developed. Joe didn't think it was working.

"It's true, Mr. Alexander," David said. "I saw a map that laid out the basics of a resort right on top of Camp Ka Nowato's land."

Mr. Alexander turned his attention from David to the two men in dark suits.

"Actually," Mr. Miller began a bit nervously, "that map is more of a corporate wish list than anything else—it shows something we would *like* to do, possibly at some point in the distant future."

It was time for Mr. French to take over. "All our stockholders know that this area is strictly considered to be under negotiation only."

"Well, I'm sorry to break the news to you," Mr. Alexander replied, "but Camp Ka Nowato is not up for any kind of negotiation. I'm sorry you made a trip out here for nothing."

"That's okay," Mr. Miller said. "As we said, we were just across the lake, anyway."

"Tom," Mr. French said, as he looked at the cafeteria. He gazed up at the old pavilion covering the weather-beaten tables and benches. Joe thought he might have even been making a quick count of all the campers. "If things don't work out for you," he continued, "I mean, if you discover that running a summer camp is not your cup of tea and you end up wanting to sell. . . ." He paused, then looked back at Mr. Alexander. "We may not be able to give you the same generous offer that we presented in the past."

Like clockwork, Mr. Miller said, "We are, after all, still running a business."

"But since we like you," Mr. French continued, "we'll give you until Friday to think it over. Three days, Tom."

Then it was Mr. Miller's turn to look around. "We'll come back then and see how you're doing."

Mr. Alexander shrugged his shoulders. "I always welcome visitors, gentlemen, but I'm telling you—I do not want to sell."

To Joe, Mr. Alexander didn't seem as sure of his answer as he had before. Joe hoped the two men from Blue Bear didn't see the indecision in Mr. Alexander's eyes that Joe had. Joe had a feeling, however, that they *had* noticed it.

"Well, just in case," Mr. French said, "we'll be back to see you on Friday." The two men made their way down the trail, toward the main road.

Joe turned his attention to Mr. Alexander and David. Mr. Alexander was watching the men from Blue Bear leave, also. He then turned to David.

"David . . ." the man said, shaking his head.

"I'm sorry, Mr. Alexander," the boy said. "I was just trying to find out more about the company."

"There's no harm done . . . I suppose," Mr. Alexander replied. He placed an arm around David's shoulder and walked back with him to the lunch line. "You just need to check with me before going into a restricted area."

Joe watched the men from Blue Bear disappear down the trail. He wondered why Mr. Alexander hadn't mentioned the pranks to the men.

Then, again, he and the others didn't have any proof Blue Bear was responsible for the pranks. And if the company wasn't the culprit, Joe guessed it was wise that Mr. Alexander hadn't said anything. Plus, if Mr. Alexander had told the men that he had been having trouble, it would have put him at a disadvantage if he did decide to sell the property. Joe hoped that he wouldn't. Something in the camp owner's eyes, however, told Joe that maybe he was considering putting up the land for sale.

Joe looked into the thick woods that surrounded the cafeteria. He honestly hoped it was Blue Bear that was pulling the pranks and that the counselors and Mr. Alexander could prove it somehow. Joe didn't want to believe there was a real ghost haunting the place. He looked into the forest a bit longer.

Either way, the pranks seemed to be making Mr. Alexander lean more toward selling the camp. If that was the case, he would probably accept the corporation's offer on Friday. That meant Joe and the other counselors had only three days to discover who was haunting the camp.

Chapter Nine

Sam sat on the aging brown-and-white horse named Scout. The large horse trotted down the dirt path that led around the east side of the lake. It was a cool Wednesday morning. She had just finished instructing her morning horseback-riding class. Her next session didn't start until after lunch.

Sam decided to take a ride to the other side of the lake before lunch. After what had happened yesterday, Blue Bear suddenly seemed to be a strong suspect. However, Sam felt that some of the strange occurrences seemed more like the kinds of pranks kids would do. It could even be kids from a competing camp, even if the competition was a thing of the past. Sam decided to pay a visit to Camp Flaming Arrow, their neighbor to the north.

She looked around as the old horse carried her slowly down the empty path. On both sides of her, tall pine trees stretched high into the sky. Their tips swayed in the morning breeze. The only sounds to be heard were the squeaking of the leather saddle and the horse's hooves as they hit the dusty path.

For thirty minutes, Sam swayed back and forth in the saddle. Then the quiet dirt path opened onto a wide asphalt road. The horse's hooves made a clomping sound as it cantered down the new road.

After a few more minutes, the road took a sharp turn to the left. Sam saw something up ahead. As horse and rider got closer, Sam saw a large sign hanging high above the road. The sign was similar to the one near the parking lot that welcomed campers to Camp Ka Nowato. Instead of hanging from two totem poles, this sign hung from two trees on either side of the road. As Sam got even closer, she saw that the sign was cut in the shape of a large arrow. Just like Camp Ka Nowato's sign, this one welcomed visitors to Camp Flaming Arrow.

Sam and Scout passed under the hanging sign, then continued down the road. As they traveled farther, Sam began to hear a faint noise in the distance. The noise sounded like a cheering crowd at a sports event. As she rode even farther, she discovered that her guess was close.

The road widened as Sam rode closer to the heart of Camp Flaming Arrow. To the right of the road, a large green field spread out in front of Sam. It was packed full of young children laughing and cheering. Some were running relay races. Others were playing kickball and other organized sports. There seemed to be dozens and dozens of campers. All of them looked as if they were having a great time.

Sam pulled gently on Scout's reins. The horse

slowly came to a stop. Sam turned her attention back from the open field to the road ahead of her. Just as at Ka Nowato, the camp's main road opened up on to a parking lot. Five brightly painted school buses were lined up side by side. Each bus was painted bright red, with the camp's name in bold yellow letters.

Sam looked past the buses and saw several wooden buildings just beyond the parking lot. They seemed to be similar in style to those at Camp Ka Nowato, except they looked almost new. They were all painted a deep green. Buildings lined the camp's main road. Sam saw several kids on horseback cross the main road after they rode out from between some of the cabins. Scout must have seen the other horses, as well. His head and ears stood straight up as he let out a small snort.

Sam looked to the left side of the road and noticed more cabins. These were closer to her, so she was able to get a close-up view of how nice they looked. Camp Flaming Arrow was what she had imagined Camp Ka Nowato would have looked like in its prime.

Sam moved the reins lightly over Scout's right shoulder. The horse reacted by turning right. He trotted on the open field. Sam decided it was time to introduce herself. She guided the horse toward the nearest camp counselor. There were plenty from which to choose. It seemed this camp had three times as many counselors as Camp Ka Nowato had.

When Sam and Scout were about fifteen feet away from the nearest group of kids, Sam pulled the reins back and Scout came to a halt. Holding onto the saddle horn, she swung her right leg around and dismounted.

Sam took the reins and led Scout the rest of the way toward the group of campers.

This particular group seemed to be enjoying an egg-carrying relay race. Each of the campers raced across the field, carrying an egg in a spoon. Sam thought the kids were doing great.

As she and Scout approached, one of the counselors broke away from the group. A girl, about the same age as Sam, walked toward her and Scout. The girl's straight brown hair was draped over her shoulders. She wore shorts and a yellow Camp Flaming Arrow T-shirt.

"May I help you?" the girl asked, when she was only a few feet away.

"Uh . . . hi," Sam said, with some hesitation. "My name is Samantha Kepler. I'm a counselor at—" She didn't get to finish.

"Camp Ka Nowato!" the other girl said excitedly. She turned her head and called over her left shoulder, "Hey, Steve!" she yelled to someone in the group behind her. "This girl is from the camp I was telling you about!"

Sam was very confused. How could this girl have possibly known. . . . As Sam suddenly looked down at the T-shirt she had on, she answered her own question. She was wearing a light blue Camp Ka Nowato T-shirt. The camp's name was printed on the shirt.

The girl turned back to Sam. "I'm sorry." She put out a hand. "My name is Patricia." Sam shook her hand. Then Patricia continued. "I was just telling Steve about Camp Ka Nowato."

A warning sign went up in Sam's mind. It seemed that Camp Ka Nowato had been the topic of recent

conversation at Camp Flaming Arrow. *If someone from this camp has been pulling pranks, maybe Patricia knows something about them,* Sam thought.

Sam watched as another counselor walked toward her and Patricia. He was slightly younger than the two girls. He looked as if he had been participating in some of the races himself. The counselor was out of breath, and beads of sweat dotted his forehead.

"Hi, I'm Steve." The counselor extended a hand to Sam. He looked at her T-shirt, puzzled. Then he turned to Patricia. "I thought you said Camp Ka Nowato had closed."

"I thought it had," Patricia replied. Both of the counselors looked directly at Sam. A questioning gaze was on both of their faces.

"It *had* closed," Sam said. "But it was just re-opened this summer."

"When we were setting up for our races earlier this morning," Patricia began, "I was telling Steve how Flaming Arrow and Ka Nowato used to compete against each other." She put a hand out and patted Scout on the head. The old horse lowered his head, as if to make it easier for Patricia to reach.

"Yes. There are photos in the camp office from some of those competitions," Sam said. She decided to probe a little. "I bet there was a big rivalry between the two camps back then."

Steve stepped up next to Scout and gave him a friendly scratch on the neck. "I don't know too much about it," Patricia said. "I've been working here only for a few summers. The inter-camp competitions were held before my time."

"This is my first summer here," Steve said. "All of us here have heard of Camp Ka Nowato, but we didn't think anyone was over there."

Patricia looked at Sam with a smile. "Do you think we could hold camp competitions again?"

"That would be great," Steve added.

"I'll ask Mr. Alexander. He's the new owner," Sam replied. "But we don't have half the number of campers you seem to have. We also have very few counselors to supervise the kids. We're just getting the old summer camp running again."

Patricia gave the horse a few more pats. Then she took a step back. "Well, let us know," she said. "We'd better get back to our group."

"Yeah," Steve said. "If we leave them alone too long, we'll have to round them up from all parts of the camp."

Sam thought that wouldn't be an easy job, now that she'd seen how many campers were attending Camp Flaming Arrow.

"It's been nice to meet you," Sam said. She placed one rein on the other side of the horse's neck. "I'll be sure and tell Mr. Alexander what you said."

"That's great," Patricia said with a wave. "Come back and visit anytime."

Sam waved, then turned toward the large horse. She inserted her left foot into the left stirrup. With a small bounce, she jumped up and threw her right leg over the horse's back. She tugged the reins to the right and Scout turned around. The old horse began to walk back to the road and head toward Camp Ka Nowato.

Sam wondered if the counselors at Camp Flaming

Arrow could be ruled out as suspects in the pranks. Even though she had talked to only two of the camp's counselors, she had a hard time believing anyone from the camp could have pulled the pranks. Both Patricia and Steve were truly surprised even to learn that the camp was open. Sam suspected the other counselors were unaware also.

Sam and Scout continued down the paved road until they came to the narrow dirt path that led back to their own summer camp. As the horse turned onto the path, Sam's mind drifted back to the previous evening.

Before she had gone to bed, Sam had read a few more chapters of *A Caribbean Mystery*. It seemed that Miss Marple had been correct about her theory that Major Palgrave's death had not been accidental. A young girl named Victoria had been working at the hotel as a maid. Victoria had made it known that the bottle of heart medication found in the major's bedroom was not his. It had not been in his room before he died. The local authorities performed an autopsy on the major. They concluded that he had been poisoned.

Like Sam and her friends, Miss Marple had a couple of suspects in mind. When the major had become nervous about showing the elderly woman the snapshot of the murderer, he was looking over her shoulder at a few arriving guests. Two of the guests were Major Greg Dyson and his wife, nicknamed Lucky.

Just like Camp Ka Nowato, the Golden Palm Hotel had been the site of more than one nasty incident.

Victoria, the maid who had found the bottle of pills, was found stabbed to death the night after the major's death. This did not look good for Major Dyson, since the pills found in Major Palgrave's room were later identified as being Major Dyson's.

Greg Dyson was not the only suspect in Miss Marple's mind, however. Among Major Palgrave's many stories, he had also mentioned poison being a woman's weapon. This fact made Miss Marple suspect Molly Kendal, one of the hotel's owners. Major Palgrave was poisoned, and Molly Kendal was the one who had found Victoria's body.

To make matters even worse, Mrs. Kendal had been having spells of memory loss. Sometimes she would not be able to remember where she had been, or what she had been doing. When she had found Victoria's body, she didn't remember what she had been doing there, as well.

Sam's mind turned back to her own mystery at camp. She believed the Caribbean mystery was almost as complicated as the one she was involved in. Sam rode on for another fifteen minutes. Her mind worked overtime as she tried to straighten out the twists and turns of both cases.

As the old horse carried her down the road, Sam heard a rustling among the trees. She immediately looked toward the noise. For a split-second, Sam saw something out of the corner of her left eye. Then, just as quickly, it was gone.

Sam immediately pulled on the reins, and Scout came to a stop. She turned the horse around and slowly had him walk back to where she had seen . . .

What *had* she seen? The image in her mind seemed unbelievable. She thought she had seen a person running through the woods. That alone was not unusual. What *was* unusual was that the person was wearing clothes made out of buckskin. That was like the clothing the native American Indians used to wear.

When Sam and Scout came to the spot where she had seen the figure, she pulled back on the reins. The old horse seemed very nervous. He kept shifting his weight from side to side. His ears were standing up perfectly straight. He even let out a small whinny, something that horse rarely did. Either he was really eager to get home, or something in those woods was spooking him.

Sam peered into the thick growth of trees. Whatever she had seen had been only about ten to twenty feet away in the forest. Some branches that the figure had run past were still even swaying back and forth. She wanted to believe that the movement of the branches could have been caused by the breeze that had been blowing all morning. But, as soon as that thought came to her, she realized the air was absolutely still.

She stared closely into the woods, searching for any sign of . . . well, anything that would prove she wasn't just imagining things. Scout let out another whinny. This one was louder than the sound he had made before. He even tried to turn back toward Camp Ka Nowato, but Sam held the reins tight. She would search a little longer.

Perhaps Sam was just imagining things. Perhaps

all her thoughts about the summer camp mystery had just made her mind play tricks on her. A small smile touched the corners of her mouth. Maybe she had even started to let the camp's legend get to her.

Sam scanned the woods one more time. That was it. She was sure she had just imagined seeing something. She began to let up on the horse's reins when her gaze fell upon something that made goose bumps break out all over her body.

Eyes.

Almost hidden behind the thick vegetation, Sam saw a pair of eyes staring at her. She couldn't believe it. She quickly moved her gaze away from the two eyes and looked at another part of the woods. She didn't want the owner of those eyes to know that she had seen them. Maybe that way she could inch the horse a little closer to the hidden watcher and get a better look at it.

Scout let out another whinny. His ears lay back as if he also sensed something watching them. Even though Sam herself was spooked, her natural sense of curiosity caused her to guide the horse closer to where she had seen the eyes. She had to be positive about what she had seen.

As horse and rider moved closer, Sam slowly turned her gaze back to the spot where she had seen the eyes. They were gone! This time she was sure she had not imagined the whole scene. She found the exact place where the eyes had been peering out at her. They were just no longer there. . . .

Sam tried to make sense of what she had just seen. She almost convinced herself that she had not seen the running figure. Sam had seen that for only the briefest time out of the corner of one eye. That could have just been her imagination. The eyes, however, had been real. She had looked right into them. And they had been looking right back at her. The thing that disturbed her most was the *kind* of eyes they were. They weren't the eyes of a bear, coyote, or any other kind of wild animal. The eyes Sam had seen were human. Some*one* was out there watching her.

Scout's fear finally got the best of him. The old horse turned toward Camp Ka Nowato and broke into a full gallop. This time Sam didn't even try to stop him. She was relieved to be heading back to her camp. Sam looked over her shoulder as she rode down the dirt path. A cloud of dust had risen into the air behind her and Scout. She was almost certain that whoever or whatever had been watching her was still there—watching.

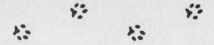

From the woods, the hidden figure watched as the girl rode down the narrow path. She had come the closest yet. She had been very, very close. For a moment, both pairs of eyes had locked gazes on each other. There was no doubt about it. She had definitely seen the eyes. The watcher would have to observe her more closely in the future.

Chapter Ten

"Come on, everybody!" Joe called to the group of youngsters. "Let's see some hustle!" Joe watched as his mid-morning basketball class ran across the court. Wishbone let out an encouraging bark, as well. Joe looked over at the dog. Wishbone was sitting on the wooden bleachers. The terrier wagged his tail when he saw Joe look his way.

Joe turned his attention back to the game. Jack Conner was in the group that Joe was coaching at the moment. Joe watched as the young boy ran down the court. At the beginning of the class, Jack had shown a great improvement from his earlier games. Joe suspected that the boy had been doing the visualization exercises he had taught him. He had been catching passes with ease, and he had even made a few baskets.

But as Jack continued to play, his performance seemed to get worse. Every time he missed a pass or a shot at the basket, Jack's confidence seemed to take a serious blow. By the end of the third drill, it was almost as if he was right back where he had started.

Joe stopped the drill and divided the group into two teams. This time, he picked the teams himself. Joe threw the basketball into the air at the faceoff, and the game was on. As Joe began to referee the game, he heard Wishbone let out a few more barks from the bleachers. For a moment, Joe thought the dog was just acting as part of the cheering section again. Then Joe realized that Wishbone was using his warning bark.

Joe looked over at Wishbone. His ears were standing straight up, and he was looking toward the trail that led to the camp's main road. Joe followed the terrier's gaze, but he saw only the empty trail. Then he heard it. A faint noise was slowly getting louder. Joe recognized the sound immediately. Anyone who had ever watched an old western would surely recognize that particular noise. It was the sound of a galloping horse. And it seemed to be coming closer.

Joe stepped away from the basketball court and walked toward the trail. The trail had a slight bend in it, so Joe couldn't see all the way to the main road. He took a few more steps. He looked down to see that Wishbone was standing by his side. The dog's eyes were fixed on the trail ahead. The galloping sound grew louder and louder.

Suddenly, a running horse burst around the curve. Joe and Wishbone stood in the shade of a tree, and the horse and rider did not see them. They almost had to dive for cover to avoid being trampled. The horse came to a sudden stop, however, then the rider pulled back tightly upon its reins. The rider was Sam!

"Joe, we have to talk right away!" she said urgently. Sam quickly dismounted. Joe thought his friend looked as if she had seen a ghost. She was pale and was breathing hard.

Joe turned back toward his players. They had all stopped their game to watch Sam's sudden arrival. "You guys keep playing," he said to the young boys. "I'll be with you in a minute."

Joe followed Sam as she led the horse toward the edge of the clearing. Whatever she had to say, she didn't want the campers to hear. Joe looked down and saw that Wishbone was still by his side. The dog was wisely keeping his distance from the horse's powerful hooves.

Joe glanced back at the basketball court. The kids had begun playing again. He turned to Sam. "What's wrong?" he asked.

Sam told Joe about her trip to Camp Flaming Arrow. She described her conversation with Patricia and Steve, the two counselors. Sam also explained why

138

she didn't think anyone from that camp should be considered a suspect.

"Maybe that does rule them out," Joe agreed. "Did anything else happen?" Joe was sure there had to be another reason why Sam had ridden so hard back down the trail.

"Well," she began, "on the way back here, I saw something. . . ." She paused for a moment, then continued. "I saw something—or someone—hiding in the woods."

"What?" Joe asked. It felt as if the temperature around the basketball area had dropped a few degrees. "Who was it?"

"I don't know," Sam replied. She continued to tell Joe about seeing the flash of buckskin and, more important, the eyes. The watching eyes. Joe felt a chill run down his spine.

"Do you think it was the person who's been pulling the pranks?" Joe asked. He hoped Sam didn't notice the shakiness in his voice.

"I don't know," she replied. "One thing is for sure—we should definitely be on the lookout and keep our eyes wide open." Sam threw one of the reins around the horse's neck as she prepared to get back up on him. "I'm going to take Scout over to the stable. Then I'll tell the other counselors what just happened."

Joe watched Sam as she climbed onto the horse's back. "Maybe it was a hiker," he told her, "or someone else camping in this area." He hoped she would agree with him.

"Maybe . . ." Sam said, as she turned the horse

around. "But I don't think so. Either way, let's keep our eyes open." She began to ride down the trail. "I'll talk to you later." Sam disappeared down the wooded trail.

Joe and Wishbone walked back to the ball court. The kids were still playing. Joe seemed to feel the temperature around him beginning to warm a little. Joe was sure that Sam had seen only a hiker or a camper. That was the best explanation. It was someone who had been startled by Sam and reacted by hiding. That was all.

There was no reason for anyone to get upset about the incident. The woods in that area stretched out for miles. There was no telling how many people came to hike or camp there. And what about the lake? The lake had to draw hundreds of tourists. What Sam had seen didn't have to be the prankster. The more Joe thought about the incident Sam described, the more he believed it could have been anybody out there in the woods.

He sat in the bleachers. Wishbone picked out a spot next to him. The dog placed a gentle paw on Joe's leg. Joe reached over and scratched him behind the ears. Joe felt uneasy. There was something bothering him. Didn't Sam say the person was wearing buckskin? And didn't the Indians of the old days wear buckskin, too? Joe didn't want to believe it, but he felt as if his superstitious nature was getting the best of him again. What if Sam had really seen . . . the ghost?

Joe immediately tried to dismiss that thought. He turned his attention back to the young camper's game. "Looking good, gang!" he said with enthusiasm, clapping his hands. He stood and walked toward the court. "Looking really good." Joe pushed all his uncomfortable thoughts toward the back of his mind. He was glad he had his basketball class to occupy him.

Joe's attention quickly turned back to Jack. The young boy was still trying very hard to overcome his feelings of insecurity. Nevertheless, it seemed that all the progress he had made over the past couple of days was quickly slipping away. There had to be something more Joe could do for Jack.

In the distance, Joe heard a loud air horn. He turned to see if he could spot the source of the noise. It sounded like one of those that belonged to an eighteen-wheeled truck. Joe heard a second blast, and then he remembered what it was. He had completely forgotten about what was planned for that day. He looked back toward his class. The boys had stopped playing and were looking at Joe.

"That's the end of the class for today," Joe announced. "Let's put the balls up. The air horn is a signal for us to stop what we are doing. Mr. Alexander has something special planned." Joe watched the kids place the basketballs into the nearby storage shed. He thought Mr. Alexander's activity would be the perfect solution for Jack's problem.

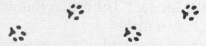

"What was that?!!" Wishbone said, as the fur on his back began to stand on end. The dog listened as the distant horn sounded a second time. "The last time I checked," he continued, "ghosts didn't make loud honking noises."

Wishbone looked over at Joe as he explained the noise to the boys. His best friend was helping the kids put away the basketballs. "I thought maybe it was a new mealtime bell," Wishbone said to himself. "After all, my stomach says it's almost lunchtime!"

The terrier followed Joe and the campers as they walked toward the main road. As he trotted behind them, his mind went back to what Sam had said. All week long, Wishbone had had the feeling he was being watched. Now, Sam had actually seen someone watching her. The terrier was glad he wasn't just imagining things. There really was someone out there in the woods watching them.

Joe, Wishbone, and the group of campers stepped onto the main road. The group continued across the road. Joe led everyone down a trail that was almost directly across from the one leading to the basketball court.

Wishbone stopped at the beginning of the second trail. "Uh . . . excuse me," Wishbone said with a bark. "Don't we need to take a left here? Toward the cafeteria? Huh . . . Joe, buddy?"

The group continued down the narrow trail.

"Hmm . . ." Wishbone said. "I guess my stomach can wait a little longer." The terrier followed the group of kids. "But only a little."

He followed Joe and his group until the trail opened up into a large clearing. Wishbone had patrolled this clearing several times, but he had never paid much attention to it. Until that moment, the dog hadn't seen anyone use that area. In fact, Wishbone didn't even know what that area was meant to be used for.

He looked ahead to see the two tall towers standing high overhead, about thirty feet apart. They were almost as tall as the pine trees that surrounded the clearing. Each tower was made of four tall poles that ran vertically in four corners. On each side of each tower, smaller poles crisscrossed to form two large X's. Each tower was a bit smaller toward the top, so the X that stood on top was a bit smaller. On top of each tower, several smaller logs had been tied tightly together to form a floor. A wooden handrail surrounded the very high platform. A ladder extended from the ground to the platform. Two large lengths of rope extended from one tower to the other. One rope was connected to the base of the platforms. The other rope was several feet above the first. It was attached to a metal pole that came up from the ground and plunged straight through the middle of each tower. At the tip of each tower, a long, thin blue triangular flag flapped in the breeze.

Wishbone craned his neck to look at the tall structures. The dog saw that, standing on the right tower, was Mr. Alexander. He was examining each of the two ropes. Wishbone lowered his gaze down to see that almost the entire population of the camp had joined them. All the kids and counselors had formed a large circle, facing the two towers. Wishbone walked over to where Joe and Jack were standing.

Joe patted Jack on the back. "This is just what you need," he said.

Wishbone saw a look of uncertainty on Jack's face.

"Hi, everybody!" Mr. Alexander called from his perch. Wishbone looked up to see the camp owner waving at the crowd. The dog gave a couple of wags of his tail in reply.

"Welcome to a very special event here at Camp Ka Nowato." Mr. Alexander was talking loudly so everyone could hear him. "This is what the ancient Chitowa Indians called a trial of confidence and trust." He looked around at the crowd, then reached up and grabbed the rope above his head. "First, we'll start with the confidence part."

Slowly, Mr. Alexander stepped onto the lower rope. Wishbone heard the rope creak as the man took the first step. The dog saw Mr. Alexander use both hands to get a firm hold on the top rope. As he held the top rope, he carefully walked across the bottom rope, and it dipped a bit in the middle from the weight. But it seemed to be anchored tightly enough not to sway back and forth under the man's weight.

Wishbone glanced at the surrounding crowd. Everyone, including Joe and Jack, seemed to be fascinated by Mr. Alexander's crossing.

"See?" the man continued. "It's very easy." He stood almost exactly at the midpoint between the two towers. "This is the confidence part. This exercise helps build self-confidence." Mr. Alexander looked at the ground below. "And now," he continued, "for the trust part. . . ."

Suddenly, Mr. Alexander's feet slipped off the rope. Wishbone heard everyone in the crowd gasp. The dog sat up instantly and watched as the man held onto the rope above him. He dangled there for a couple of seconds, then let go and began to fall to the ground. Wishbone barked, and a few of the younger campers screamed with fright.

Then, suddenly, Mr. Alexander stopped falling. He simply floated there between the lower rope and the ground. Then Wishbone saw something he hadn't noticed before. Mr. Alexander was wearing a black-leather harness around his waist and shoulders. From the harness, a dark length of rope extended straight up. The summer camp's director was dangling from a third rope!

Wishbone followed the safety rope to see that it looped through a metal ring. The ring was attached to a thick metal cable that was suspended high above the two ropes. Wishbone followed the cable to see that it was attached to the two metal poles that extended through the towers. The dog couldn't believe he hadn't seen it before; after all, he had great eyesight.

Wishbone continued to follow the safety rope with his sharp eyes. After it passed through the metal ring, it dropped to the ground, to the edge of the clearing. Holding onto the other end of the rope was Barry. He was wearing a similar harness. The rope seemed to be attached to his harness somehow. Wishbone also noticed that the back of Barry's harness was tied to a large tree.

Barry slowly worked his hands back and forth along the rope. Wishbone turned back to face the center of the clearing. Barry was slowly lowering Mr. Alexander to the ground. Wishbone wagged his tail. "What a cool trick," he said. "For a second there, I thought we would have to find ourselves a new camp director."

Mr. Alexander planted his feet gently on the ground. All the campers seemed to be as relieved as Wishbone was.

146

"So there you have it," Mr. Alexander said. He didn't have to speak as loudly as before. "This exercise is perfectly safe—thanks to Barry, over there." The man gestured to Barry, who gave a theatrical bow. "Now," Mr. Alexander continued, "anyone who wants to do this, please form one line over there." He pointed to the tower at Wishbone's right. "You don't have to do it. But I highly recommend it." He gave a boyish smile. "It's really a lot of fun!"

Soon, the first camper was harnessed and atop the first tower. Wishbone watched as the camper, a young girl, walked slowly across the rope between the two towers. Mr. Alexander stood atop the first tower, and Sam had positioned herself on the second one. Their purpose was to look out for the young camper's safety. Both of them wore safety harnesses that were attached to the towers themselves.

The girl was about halfway across when, suddenly, both her feet slipped off the bottom rope. The crowd on the ground let out a small gasp. Holding tightly to the top rope, the young girl quickly placed her feet back onto the bottom rope. Wishbone was relieved. The girl then quickly shuffled to the other side. Sam helped her down the ladder.

Rebecca, David, and Joe helped each of the other campers into the safety harness. Each camper would then climb one of the towers. When they reached the platform, they would strap on Barry's safety rope.

Everyone seemed to be having a great time. The entire group cheered after someone successfully made his or her way across the rope. Wishbone helped by letting out a bark or two with each cheer. Only a couple of campers slipped and had to be lowered down by Barry. All in all, Joe saw that everyone really enjoyed the activity . . . everyone except for Jack.

While all the other campers were walking across the rope, Jack stood at the back of the line with a worried expression. Finally, it was his turn to do the exercise. Joe helped him put his harness on.

"You'll do just fine, Jack," Joe said to the nervous-looking boy.

When his harness was in place, Jack put his hands on the ladder. Shakily and slowly, the boy climbed up the tower. When Jack was about halfway up, however, he stopped and looked around. For a long moment he seemed frozen in place. Then he came back down. It was clear Jack was too frightened to continue.

Some of the other kids started to laugh at him. Mr. Alexander quickly spoke up. "Now, remember, kids," he said, "this exercise isn't for everybody. In fact, it took me *five* tries before I worked up the courage to get on this thing." The crowd laughed and the camp owner continued. "Let's all give Jack a big round of applause for trying!"

Everyone clapped as Jack stepped onto the ground. The boy smiled a little, but Wishbone could see he was embarrassed.

"That's okay," Joe told Jack, as he helped him remove the safety harness. "You don't have to do the exercise if you don't want to." Joe smiled and patted him on the back. Wishbone could tell that Joe was disappointed. He knew that Joe had hoped this exercise would help Jack improve his sense of self-confidence. Maybe Joe could find some other way to give the young camper the psychological boost he needed.

Wishbone walked over to Jack and sat up on his hind legs. "Don't worry," the dog said, his tongue hanging out of his mouth a bit. "You wouldn't catch this dog on that thing." Wishbone let out a small bark. "And I'm the bravest dog I know!"

Wishbone got back on all fours and gazed into the surrounding forest. He thought back to what Sam had said. He wondered if anyone was watching them now.

"Did I said *bravest?*"

Chapter Eleven

For the rest of the day, Wishbone set his guard-dog mode on maximum alert. If there was someone sneaking around in the woods, he was going to sniff out the culprit! Wishbone tripled his rounds, checking everything six times instead of two. The dog was careful to examine every area of the camp very, very thoroughly. Unfortunately, his super-sensitive nose didn't discover anything but the usual smells—pine needles, the typical forest animals, and that camp smell he still couldn't put his paw on.

After dinner that evening, the camp members had gathered at the council ring to hear some spooky stories and sing songs. It was the perfect night for it, too. A strong wind made the treetops bend and sway.

Wishbone loved to hear spooky stories. Under any other circumstances, he would have sat and listened with the group. However, he couldn't afford to let himself relax. While everyone was gathered to-gether, Wishbone dutifully patrolled the outside of the council ring. He had to make absolutely sure the perimeter was secure.

When the camp's story time was over, everyone returned to their cabins and got ready to go to sleep. More than anyone, Wishbone was ready for a good night's rest. He never realized that being head of camp security could make him feel so dog-tired. The terrier made one more quick check of the entire camp before calling it a night. Once again, for what seemed like the gazillionth time, Wishbone didn't find anything out of the ordinary. Satisfied that all was well, he slowly dragged his tired body back to Joe and David's cabin. It was time for some long-awaited sleep.

Wishbone nosed open the door, which hadn't been closed all the way. He made his way through the small opening. Joe and David were already fast asleep. David had even begun to snore a little. Carefully and quietly, Wishbone crawled up onto the foot of Joe's bed. He didn't want to wake up his buddy. He just wanted to get comfortable and fall asleep as soon as possible.

Wishbone circled twice, then lightly pawed at the blanket. After adjusting the spot for maximum comfort, he curled up next to Joe's feet. He let out a deep breath, then closed his eyes.

Slowly, Wishbone began to drift off into dream-land. He was only slightly aware of the world beyond the camp. He could hear the strong wind blow through the trees outside the cabin. Inside, he heard David's light snoring. He also heard himself breathing in slow, long, even breaths. The dog went into a deeper and deeper sleep. As the world slowly closed to a black silence, Wishbone was able to hear his own heart, beating slowly.

Wishbone then slowly began to wake up from his sleep. Joe had moved his legs and sat up in bed. Wishbone knew he wasn't completely awake, because he could still hear the slow beating of his own heart.

"David," Joe whispered. "David!"

"Yeah?" a groggy David replied.

"Do you hear that?" Joe said a bit louder. "What is that beating noise?"

Wishbone was slowly going back to sleep. He thought about what Joe had just said. "That's funny, Joe," the dog mumbled in his sleepy state. "You can hear my heart beating, too." Wishbone paused a second. Then his head popped straight up. He was completely awake now. "You can hear *my* heart beat?" Wishbone could still hear the beating. It was a very deep and low sound.

Beat . . . beat . . . beat . . . beat . . .

"It sounds like a drum," David said. "A Native American drum."

Wishbone sensed that Joe felt a bit uneasy. David immediately began to get out of bed. Joe seemed to hesitate at first, but finally he, too, pulled the blanket off himself and put on his sneakers. Both of the boys were wearing sweatpants and T-shirts. Joe got his flashlight from his storage cabinet.

David reached into his cabinet and grabbed a flashlight. "Let's check it out," he said.

Wishbone saw a bit of excitement in David's eyes. The dog looked at Joe, but saw only a worried expression.

Joe, David, and Wishbone slowly walked outside the cabin. Both boys had their flashlights on. Almost at once, Wishbone heard a rustling noise coming from

the woods. David aimed his flashlight beam at the spot where the noise came from. After a moment, they saw Sam walking quickly toward them. The woods between the cabins weren't as thick as the ones around the rest of the camp.

"What is that sound?" she asked. Sam was wearing an oversized T-shirt and sweatpants. Wishbone noticed that a couple of leaves were stuck in her hair.

"I have no idea," Joe answered. "We just heard it ourselves."

The noise continued in low, steady beats. It sounded as if it was coming from the south side of the camp. There, the woods were the thickest and the trails were the narrowest.

From the opposite direction, Wishbone began to hear the stirring of several of the campers. The dog cocked his head to tune into their voices. Several of them were asking what was going on. Others were saying the beating was Ka Nowato's ghost. Wishbone even heard one little girl crying.

Sam must have heard some of the campers, as well. "Joe, David, you two go check out what's going on out there," she said. "I'm going to get the other counselors and try to calm down the kids."

David agreed. He began to walk down a trail leading toward the south side of the camp. Wishbone took off after him. The dog looked over his shoulder to see Joe pause a moment, then quickly follow. Wishbone knew Joe still felt uneasy.

"It'll be okay, Joe," the dog called back. Wishbone ran past David and down the dark trail. "But right now, I've got a ghost to catch!"

David watched as Wishbone passed him and ran down the trail, away from the cabins. The terrier trotted through the light created by his flashlight beam and then disappeared into the darkness. David began to run. Behind him, he heard Joe's footsteps on the narrow trail.

As they ran deeper into the dark woods, the beating sounded stronger and more haunting.

"Where is it coming from?" Joe asked.

"The sound's frequency is so low," David answered. "It's hard to tell."

They continued on the dark trail. The drumbeat was getting louder and louder. They had to be getting close to the sound's source. Then, the wind blew and the noise sounded as if it had moved behind them.

"What the—" said Joe.

David was about to turn around when he heard a noise ahead of him. He moved his flashlight beam until it faded into the darkness of the trail. Then a white object came into view. It was Wishbone. Apparently, the dog had heard the sound shift behind them as well. Wishbone ran past Joe and David. David turned to watch him run back toward the cabins.

"Come on," David said, as he took off after him. He and Joe ran side by side up the dark trail. Their two flashlight beams danced across the passing trees.

They came upon the beginning of another trail heading east. The drumbeat now sounded as if was coming from that direction. Joe and David took a right, toward the sound. They ran down the dark trail, and the beating grew louder. Then, as Joe and David seemed to be right on top of the mysterious sound, it shifted again. It sounded as if it had moved behind them again.

David stopped running and turned around. "This is too weird," he said to Joe.

"What could possibly—" Joe started to say, but he quickly stopped. He shone his flashlight down the trail in front of them. Once again, Wishbone came running in the opposite direction, heading west. He passed them and continued toward the beating drum's new position.

"It looks like we're not the only ones who are confused," said David.

The two boys followed the terrier once again. They continued past the trail that they had originally started on. It ran north and south. The drumbeat now seemed to be coming from the west. They ran toward the sound and stopped when they saw Wishbone standing right in the middle of the trail. The dog had his nose pointed up in the air. He looked as if he were trying to pick up a scent. David thought the strong wind was probably interfering with Wishbone's search. He couldn't seem to get a solid lead because the breeze was moving the sound from one place to another within seconds.

David and Joe stood beside the sniffing dog. They each shone their flashlights into the surrounding woods. The wind made it harder to pinpoint the source of the sound. But the drumming sounded as if it was coming from a spot just off the trail. In fact, David estimated it could be no more than twenty feet away to their left. He and Joe peered into the dark woods. Unfortunately, their flashlights didn't detect anything that could have been making the noise.

Beat . . . beat . . . beat . . . beat . . .

The wind shifted again and the drumbeat sounded as if it were coming from the opposite direction again. David couldn't understand how that was possible. He knew that there had to be a logical explanation for the sound appearing to change directions. But the drumbeat's change in position shifted so dramatically that it couldn't have been due to the wind's effect alone.

Beat . . . beat . . . beat . . . beat . . .

"Uh . . . I don't know about this," Joe said.

David heard a nervousness in his friend's voice. David was beginning to feel frightened, as well. All his scientific theories and knowledge seemed to fly right out the window. He tried to think about some rational scientific reasons to explain what was happening, but the only thought that kept running through his mind was the idea of the ghost.

Beat . . . beat . . . beat . . . beat . . .

The beats were so loud that it sounded as if the boys and the dog had been placed inside the drum itself.

Beat . . . beat . . .

The steady beat stopped. Suddenly, there was nothing but absolute silence. David thought the wind even seemed to stop blowing. He, Joe, and Wishbone stood there, frozen. The woods were so still that they almost seemed spookier than when the drumbeats had echoed through them. The three stood there a moment longer.

"What just happened?" Joe asked. He began to shine his flashlight around again.

"I'm not sure," David replied. He, too, began to move his light around. The bright circle of light passed through the silent trees. He looked down at Wishbone. The dog had begun to sniff the ground again.

"We'd better get back to the others," Joe said.

"I guess so," David replied.

The two boys began to walk back toward their cabin. David saw that Wishbone had given up his search, as well. The dog trotted along behind them.

On the way back, David tried to make sense of what had just happened. Unfortunately, he found that he couldn't. Before he had come to Camp Ka Nowato, David firmly believed there was no such thing as a ghost. Although he really didn't want to admit it now, that belief was no longer so clear-cut.

So many odd events had occurred in such a short time. What possible rational reason could have been behind all the strange happenings? There had been a ghostly sighting made by Joe at the abandoned campsite. There had been all the vandalism. There had been Sam's sighting of the buckskin-clad figure in the woods. David couldn't even explain why none of his computer software seemed to have worked in the camp office.

David added the spooky drumbeat to the list of creepy occurrences. He admitted that if someone wanted to sit in the woods and beat a large drum, the person could produce a very spooky noise. But the way the beat seemed to float around them was impossible to explain in a logical, scientific way. David didn't think the wind's effect on the drum's sound waves would create those weird effects.

The three continued up the dark trail until they were almost back at the cabins. As David began to see the light of the lampposts through the thick forest, he heard a noise on the trail behind them. He glanced back and was startled to see Rebecca and Jeremy only a few feet behind him, Joe, and Wishbone.

"Did you find anything?" Rebecca asked.

Joe turned around quickly. He also seemed startled by her voice. "Where did you come from?" Joe

asked, as he looked from Rebecca to Jeremy. He and David stopped walking.

"We came up the west trail," Jeremy answered. "We were hoping to come around the other side of whoever has been making that drumbeat noise."

"Or *whatever* was making the noise," Rebecca added. "That was pretty spooky, huh?"

David noticed a small gleam in the girl's eyes. He wondered if she was one of those people who enjoyed being a little scared.

"We didn't see anything," Joe said. "Nothing at all." To David, Joe seemed a little annoyed by Rebecca's reaction.

Jeremy started to walk down the trail toward the cabins. "We'd better see about the campers," he said. "I'm sure Barry and Sam can't handle the entire group for long. They are probably anxious to hear some news about what we discovered."

David, Joe, and Rebecca agreed and quickly followed Jeremy. Wishbone was right behind them.

David stopped for a moment. Then he continued down the trail behind the rest of the group. Something bothered him. He thought it was kind of suspicious for the brother and sister to appear out of nowhere the way they had. They could have been telling the truth, he supposed. Their story about going down the other trail actually made sense. However, something about the situation still bothered him.

After walking in silence for a short distance, David realized what was eating at him. It was the silence itself. When the drumbeat had stopped, everything had gotten very quiet. There was something about that stillness that nagged at his mind. David followed the group for a few more feet. They were almost at the first group of cabins. He could see that a few of the campers were standing outside their cabins.

It wasn't the silence, David thought. *It was right before the silence!* David stopped walking and let the group continue alone up the path. He thought back to the last time they had heard the drumbeats. They had been very loud. The drumbeats seemed as if they had been coming from all around. Then, they suddenly stopped. Suddenly? David closed his eyes and thought back for a moment. The beats hadn't stopped suddenly. There had been an echo of some kind. No, that wasn't quite right. There had been the last drumbeat, then a half-beat. It sounded as if someone had started to beat the drum, then stopped during mid-beat.

The half-beat wouldn't have been so strange, except for one thing. Near the end, the beating sounded as if it were coming from all around them. The last half-beat sounded as if it were coming from behind them only. David thought a bit harder. What if there had been more than one drum beating? If two drums had been beating at the same time, wouldn't it have sounded like just one drum? And if the two drums were on opposite sides of a person, wouldn't it sound as if one drum was beating all around them? Yes. Yes, it would.

David continued up the trail. He realized he didn't have any solid evidence to prove any of his theory. But one thing was certain—he planned to keep a very close eye on Rebecca and Jeremy.

Chapter Twelve

"Some guard dog *I* turned out to be," Wishbone said, as he trotted down the camp's main road. It was almost lunchtime on Thursday. The terrier hung his head as he went toward the cafeteria. At first, when the strange events had started to take place, Wishbone thought he might be letting everyone down when he couldn't figure out who—or what—the culprit was. Now he knew for sure that he was disappointing people.

The night before, he, Joe, and David had gone on a wild-goose chase. The dog had tried his very best to track down whoever was making that drum noise, but he couldn't. He'd tried to sniff out the culprit, but it had been too windy to catch a good scent. He'd tried to follow the sound, but it kept moving. He was supposed to be the camp's ace guard dog. But he was turning out to be a failure.

To make matters even worse, later that night, two more canoes had been vandalized. Even more serious than that, however, was the fact that the food-storage lockers had been broken into again. Once again, Wishbone and Barry had found bits and pieces of food and plastic bags scattered all around the cafeteria. The wild animals must have thought it was another free, all-you-can-eat buffet.

The dog trotted past the trail that led to the archery range. He had already made his third guard-dog round of the day. Earlier that morning, Joe and David had told Mr. Alexander what had happened the previous night. Sam had also explained to the camp's owner about her experience on the ride back from the other summer camp.

Mr. Alexander seemed quite disturbed about the events that had been occurring during the first week that his summer camp was in operation. The dog had decided not to disappoint the camp's owner any more than he already had. Wishbone had decided to add two extra passes to his morning rounds.

The saddened dog came over a hill and saw that everyone was eating lunch. Normally, Wishbone was one of the first ones in line. That day, however, he didn't feel much like eating. That was a very unusual feeling for him to have. He took in a deep sniff. Salisbury steak. Wishbone loved Salisbury steak. He finally decided that eating a little bit of lunch might not be such a bad idea.

Wishbone walked under the cafeteria's pavilion roof. He saw that all the counselors and Mr. Alexander were sitting at a table together. They looked as if they had already finished eating. Usually, the counselors split up and sat and ate with the young campers. If the older kids were sitting together, Wishbone thought something unusual had to be going on. The dog trotted over and sat on the ground next to Joe. He decided the Salisbury steak could wait.

"I'm not sure what to do, everyone," Mr. Alexander said. "Things are not turning out at all the way I expected."

"Doesn't this incident add excitement to the camp legend and help make it even more popular?" Rebecca asked.

Wishbone thought she was just trying to be optimistic.

"*Help?*" Mr. Alexander said. "How do holes in the canoes or ruined food help?"

"I think it helps the camp legend *too* much," Sam added. "Some of the campers are really getting scared."

Mr. Alexander shook his head. "I'm sorry," he said. "This entire situation is really starting to have a bad effect on me. I'm starting to think Blue Bear's offer is looking pretty good."

"But what if Blue Bear is the one pulling the pranks?" Joe asked. "If you decide to sell the camp to them, you'll be letting them win."

"I don't know . . ." the camp's owner replied. "Maybe they *have* won. And if they're *not* the ones responsible for the vandalism"—he took a sip from his mug—"let the ghost of Ka Nowato be *their* problem."

Wishbone looked around to see the faces of all the counselors sitting at the table. All of them looked shocked. Wishbone thought they probably felt the same way he did. Over the past four and a half days, he had come to think of Camp Ka Nowato as a second home. He had grown quite attached to the place. By the expressions on everyone's face, it seemed they felt the same way.

"Don't worry," Mr. Alexander said to the counselors. "I'm not running to the phone to call Blue Bear just yet." He stood up and picked up his lunch tray. "I'll head back to the office and try to figure out some alternative." He walked toward the serving area and emptied his tray into a large trash can.

Wishbone watched as the camp's owner walked slowly down the short trail leading to the main road.

"What are we going to do?" Sam asked. "We can't just stand by and watch Mr. Alexander lose the camp."

"If Blue Bear is trying to scare everyone away, what *can* we do?" Joe asked.

"I think Mr. Alexander is making too big a deal of the whole thing," Jeremy said, as he poked at his lunch with a fork.

Wishbone's stomach gave a small growl. "Hang on, stomach," Wishbone said. "Business first, food later."

Jeremy continued. "I agree with Rebecca. I think everything that's happened just adds to the camp's legend. It will pull *in* customers in the long run."

"What if there is no long run?" Barry asked. "What if we have to close the camp after this week?" He looked around the table. "I've known Mr. Alexander for a long time, and I've never seen him this upset about anything."

"He's right," David said. "The men from Blue Bear are coming back tomorrow. We have to do something—and fast."

Wishbone noticed a small smile come across Sam's lips. It looked as if she had an idea. "I know," she said. "Something strange has happened every night this week, right?" All the other counselors shook their heads in agreement. "Well, I say tonight we go on a stakeout."

"What a great idea!" Wishbone said with a bark.

"We can all hide near the places that have gotten vandalized." Sam looked at Rebecca, then at the others. "Rebecca and I can hide in the safety tower and watch over the canoes." She turned to Joe. "Joe and Jeremy can hide out by the food-storage lockers." Sam looked at David. "David and Barry can stake out the campsite across the bridge."

"That's a great idea, Sam," Joe said. He turned to David and the others. "What do you think?"

"I agree," David said. "With all of us on high alert, we're bound to see something."

"I think it's a good idea, too," Barry said. "Let's meet back here thirty minutes after lights-out tonight." He looked over his shoulder at the campers. "That will give everyone a chance to go to sleep before we start our work."

Everyone else agreed. Wishbone stood up on all fours. "By the power given to me as camp security chief"—he let out a small bark—"I hereby deputize each of you for special guard duty!" The dog returned to a sitting position and barked again. "Now," he said, "would one of you please be so kind as to feed your security chief?"

After seeing Wishbone sit, Joe picked up a small piece of leftover Salisbury steak from his tray and gave it to the terrier. Wishbone gobbled it down.

"That's a great start, Joe," the terrier said. "Now, can you find me a piece with just a little more gravy on it?"

That night, David met Joe and Sam on the camp's main road. All the campers had already gone to bed. David, Joe, and Sam had decided to get together before meeting with Jeremy, Rebecca, and Barry. They began to walk toward the cafeteria. Wishbone also joined them.

"So," Sam began, "are you two thinking what I am thinking?"

David answered. "If you're thinking of adding another suspect to the list, so am I."

"*Two* more suspects," Joe said.

"That was a good idea you had to split up Jeremy and Rebecca like that, Sam," David said.

"I'm just glad I'm not the only one who has been suspecting them," she answered. "It seems fishy how they keep showing up at the scene right after a spooky event has just happened."

"Remember how they were beating the drums in the opening ceremonies?" David asked. "There were drums involved at *both* ghostly incidents."

"Why would they want to put Mr. Alexander out of business?" Joe asked.

"I don't know," David answered. "But I'm sure about one thing—something strange has happened every night we have been here. If Jeremy or Rebecca tries anything sneaky, one of us will be there to see it."

As the cafeteria came into view, Wishbone ran ahead of his three friends and began to sniff out the area. David was able to see Barry, Jeremy, and Rebecca sitting under the pavilion's lights.

Before David, Joe, and Sam were close enough for the others to hear them, David asked another question. "What about Barry? Did either of you ever think *he* might be involved in the pranks?"

"I don't know," Sam said. "He seems to be pretty good friends with Mr. Alexander."

"Sam's right," Joe agreed. "I can't see any reason why he would want to put Mr. Alexander out of business."

David thought about that for a moment. "I suppose you're right," he said. "Either way, I'll be there to keep an eye on him—just in case."

David, Sam, and Joe met the other counselors under the cafeteria's pavilion. David saw that Wishbone was sniffing along the ground. He thought the dog might be looking for any suspicious crumbs that needed to be examined more closely. A smile came to his lips at the thought.

After an exchange of greetings, the group of counselors split up into pairs. Joe, Wishbone, and Jeremy walked out into the woods to get a good look at the food-storage lockers. The other four continued down the main road until it forked in two directions. Sam and Rebecca walked up the trail leading to the boat docks. David and Barry walked down the narrower trail, which led to the old bridge and the abandoned campsite across the way.

When David and Barry got to the bridge, they

carefully shone their flashlights downward as a guide for every step they took. They were careful not to walk on any part of the bridge where the wood might have rotted through. The old bridge creaked steadily under their weight, but both of them made it across safely.

Once on the other side of the bridge, David and Barry climbed the small hill to the old abandoned campsite. When they reached the top, they moved their flashlights around to shine on the old, empty cabins.

"Let's hide in that cabin there." Barry pointed to a cabin that was very close to the center of the campsite.

"Perfect," David replied.

The two counselors walked over to the old cabin. David pulled the door open slowly. It scraped along the ground, moving a small mound of pine needles aside. When the door was completely open, both David and Barry aimed their flashlights inside. The place was completely empty. The cabin contained a few cobwebs and what looked like an abandoned rat's

nest; otherwise, it didn't seem to be in bad shape. David thought the inside had held up a lot better than the outside had.

Once the boys had gone inside, Barry closed the door. Each of the two counselors took up a position by each of the two front windows.

"I wonder how long we'll have to wait for some action," David said.

"I don't know," Barry replied. He opened the window he was standing at. A cloud of dust flew off it. Barry waved the dust out of his face. He turned off his flashlight. "I hope it's not too long," he said. "This isn't exactly what I had in mind when I decided I wanted to be a camp counselor this summer."

David laughed and turned off his flashlight, as well. A quarter-moon helped David to scan the empty campground. There was no movement outside at all. Only a slight breeze seemed to make the treetops sway. As David looked outside at the area, his eyes fell upon the spot where Joe had seen the ghostly campfire. The ground looked normal. There wasn't a scorch mark of any kind. Joe had said a large column of blue flame had shot from the middle of the fire. That reminded David of the camp's opening ceremony. There, a column of *smoke* had burst from the campfire.

David shifted his gaze from the campground to the trees above. He could see the night sky through the swaying treetops. The quarter-moon peeked through and cast light upon the moving leaves. David squinted and thought he saw something else in the trees. A small, dark object swayed back and forth, as well.

David reached for his flashlight. He was about to turn it on to get a better look when he was suddenly distracted. From across the lake's inlet, he heard a very loud splash. . . .

Chapter Thirteen

Sam and Rebecca had taken a right turn at the two trails that forked off from the main road. The two girls walked down the trail toward the boat docks. They passed the storage shed and the rows of canoes stacked on racks. The three piers stretched out from the water's edge. On top of the one on the far right, the safety tower stood on four tall wooden stilts.

The two girls shone their flashlights as they climbed to the top of the ladder and then stepped through the high doorway. The small tower room was completely empty. Narrow, open windows lined each of the walls. Each window was only about six inches wide, but together, they ran around the entire room. A cool breeze blew through them as water lapped against the docks below.

Sam and Rebecca sat on the floor, their backs against the wall. Rebecca let out a large sigh. "I really don't see the point of this stakeout," she said.

"Whoever is pulling the pranks isn't going to do anything if they discover we're watching over everything. It just seems a complete waste of time."

"Could be," Sam replied. *Especially if the pranksters happen to be teamed up with people who can keep an eye on them,* she thought.

The two girls sat quietly for a few minutes. Occasionally, Sam would stand and look out one of the windows or the doorway. Rebecca didn't seem interested in being there at all. She just shifted back and forth on the floor. Sam couldn't even strike up a conversation with her.

"I'm going to get a soft drink from the cafeteria," Rebecca said finally. She stood up. "Do you want anything?" she asked Sam.

"I'm okay," Sam replied.

"I'll be right back," Rebecca said, as she neared the open doorway. She walked out and climbed down the ladder.

As Sam watched her go, she wondered if Jeremy was making the same excuse. Sam stood up and looked through one of the windows as Rebecca cut through the woods toward the cafeteria. When the girl disappeared from view, Sam leaned back against a wall. She supposed Joe would see Rebecca approaching and keep an eye on her. Besides, if she didn't come back in a few minutes, Sam would go to look for her.

Sam sat against the wall of the tower and enjoyed the cool breeze coming off the lake. The smell of moisture in the air made her think of Miss Marple at the Golden Palm Hotel. A local police official had been called in to investigate the murders of both Major

Palgrave and the maid, Victoria. The police official soon discovered that Greg Dyson, Miss Marple's prime suspect, had married his current wife, Lucky, after his first wife had died. Lucky had been the nurse of Dyson's first wife. That placed Dyson, and possibly Lucky, at the top of the suspect list. Nevertheless, there was still no real evidence against him.

However, Mr. Dyson was not Miss Marple's only suspect. The other one was the co-owner of the hotel, Molly Kendal. Mrs. Kendal's behavior had seemed to be worsening. She even appeared to have attempted to kill herself. In the state of mind she was in, there was no telling what Mrs. Kendal was capable of.

Before Sam had gone to meet Joe and David that evening, she had had a chance to read a little more of *A Caribbean Mystery*. She had left off at an exciting part of the story. It seemed that Dyson's wife, Lucky, had just died in a swimming accident. However, Miss Marple thought the unfortunate incident might be another clue to solving the case.

Sam was suddenly shaken out of her thoughts. The entire tower seemed to rock to one side. She tried to stand, but another violent shaking of the tower knocked her back to the floor. Sam immediately placed her hand on the windowsill above her. As she pulled herself up, there came another fierce blow to the tower. This time, the entire floor seemed to be swept right out from under her.

The tower leaned dangerously at an angle out over the water. Sam tried to scramble to the open doorway. Instead, the tower leaned out farther. Sam reached for the tilted floor. It was like trying to climb

up a slide backward. Her legs kicked desperately as she tried to crawl upward toward the door.

There was another sharp blow. Sam felt the tower break free from the stilts below. She looked through the doorway and saw the treetops disappear from view as the tower fell into the lake.

Splash!!!

Sam was thrown back against the far wall as the tower slammed into the lake. The fall knocked the wind out of her for a moment. Then Sam saw water begin to pour through the opened windows. The tiny room began to sink. As it did, Sam tried desperately to clear her thoughts. The windows were too narrow for her to climb through. Sam's only hope of escaping from the quickly sinking structure would be to crawl through the doorway, which was still above the waterline.

Since the room was now sinking into the water backward, the doorway was directly overhead. As the tower sank, the opening got closer and closer to the water. The water level was rising fast. Sam soon realized she would have to tread water to keep from drowning. She planned to tread water until the doorway was within reach.

Sam swam inside the sinking tower. The only light came from the moonlight that threw a dim glow into the doorway, above her. And the doorway was quickly getting closer to Sam. When it was within reach, Sam kicked hard and pushed herself out of the water. With one hand, she grabbed onto one side of the door frame. But when Sam put her full weight on the door frame, that side of the room was pulled down even closer to the water. Since the sinking tower was no longer attached to anything, the room tipped back and forth until the door was completely underwater. Sam saw that she was trapped.

Water flowed into the open window that was now above her. Sam grabbed onto the window's frame in a desperate move to stay above the water. But it didn't work. The room was sinking fast. The tower was sticking out of the water only a few inches by then. Sam pulled her face up to the narrow opening to gasp for breath.

Sam knew the doorway was her only chance to escape. With the tower almost completely underwater, she held her face toward the open window. Sam took in a deep breath, then pushed away as hard as she could. Once completely underwater, she swam toward the open doorway. She couldn't see anything in the dark, murky lake water. Sam swam in the general direction of the doorway. Her lungs felt tight as she kicked deeper underwater. She hoped she could hold her breath as long as she needed to.

Suddenly, her hands touched the hard surface of the tower's opposite wall. Sam hovered there as she felt around for the open doorway. Her lungs began to ache. After what seemed like forever, she found it. Her hands ran across the open frame of the doorway. With lungs that felt as if they were going to burst, Sam grabbed the frame with both hands. She quickly pulled herself through the open doorway. After she kicked her legs with all her strength and made it through the opening, Sam swam frantically toward the surface, feeling herself fade out even as she swam.

Chapter Fourteen

Wishbone sat quietly in the bushes. He was keeping a close watch on the food-storage lockers. He was glad Joe had decided to stand guard over that area. That way, the dog could do two of his favorite things at once—he could spend time with his best friend, and he got to stand guard over the most important part of the summer camp.

So far, the evening had been fairly calm. He and Joe had been startled earlier by Rebecca. She had come to the cafeteria to get something, probably a snack, from the refrigerated storage locker. Even though the locker's walls were thickly insulated, Wishbone had heard the girl rummaging around in there.

The dog stood and took a couple of steps toward the locker. "Maybe she needs some help," the dog said, as he took another step. "I would be failing in my security duties if I didn't help her . . ."—he gave a small cough—". . . help her in any way."

Wishbone had worked his way almost to the door

of the locker when he heard a distant cracking noise. The dog turned his head and cocked it to one side. The distant sound was soon followed by loud splash. "Trouble!" Wishbone said, and he ran into the woods. From behind him, he heard Joe and Jeremy's footsteps.

Earlier, Wishbone had watched Rebecca approach the cafeteria area through a very narrow trail that led up from the boat docks. Wishbone was running down that trail now. He jumped over large rocks and ducked under low tree branches. Wishbone wasn't sure what that sound had been, but he was sure it wasn't a good sign. Maybe he and his partners would finally catch that creepy ghost in the act of committing yet another prank.

When Wishbone could finally see the docks through the trees, something didn't look right. He had to get a little closer before he could tell exactly what it was. When the dog was within just a few feet of the area, his fur bristled when he saw what awaited him. The tower was gone. Only four cracked and splintered bases of the wooden posts stood on the pier where the tower used to be.

Wishbone headed straight for the now empty dock. He ran onto the wooden pier and looked at the dark water beyond. The water was very choppy just off the edge of the pier. In the pale moonlight that hit the surface of the water, Wishbone saw bubbles rising. To the dog, it looked as if the tower had fallen into the water and sunk. What if Sam was still in there?

Wishbone turned toward the woods and barked loudly and continuously. He knew he had outrun Joe and Jeremy on the way there. Now he had to let them know there was real trouble. Sam was not with Rebecca; so she must still be in the tower. Wishbone realized she was *trapped* underwater!

"Come on, Joe!" Wishbone yelled. He continued to bark with no letup. "Sam is in really big trouble!" Wishbone ran back to the edge of the forest. He heard the two boys coming through the thick woods. They were close, but not close enough. If they were going to rescue Sam from the water, they could not waste any time.

Wishbone ran to the water to dive in himself, when he heard a moaning sound. He turned to his right and saw a figure stretched out across the sandy bank just a few feet from the water's edge. Wishbone took a couple of steps closer, and he saw that it was Sam! The dog ran over to the girl. She was soaking wet and seemed to be a bit dazed. When he got to her, she started to cough and sat up slowly.

"Are you all right, Sam?" Wishbone said, as he gave her hand two small licks. Wishbone turned to see Joe and Jeremy come out from the woods. The dog gave a couple of barks, and the boys' flashlight beams immediately aimed in his direction. The lights blinded him for a moment. He turned his head away.

When he turned his head back toward the lights, Wishbone saw two more flashlight beams coming from another direction. The dog was about to bark another signal of alert when he saw it was David and Barry. All four of the counselors came over to Sam at almost the same time. Wishbone heard them all ask, "What happened?" and "Are you okay?"

"I'm not sure *what* happened," Sam said between

coughs. "Rebecca had left to get a soft drink at the cafeteria. Shortly after, I was inside the tower when it suddenly started to rock back and forth. I was about to try to see who was doing it when the whole thing toppled over and went crashing into the lake." She looked around at the concerned group. Wishbone thought she still seemed a bit disoriented. "I was trapped inside the tower as it started to sink." She coughed again. "It all happened so quickly."

"How did you get out?" David asked.

"I swam out through the doorway, but by that time I was almost out of breath," she answered. Sam slowly tried to get to her feet. David and Joe grabbed her arms and helped her. She coughed a little more. "Someone grabbed me just as I was about to go under and helped me swim to shore." She looked at the others. "Was it one of you?"

"We all just got here," Joe said.

"What's that?" Jeremy asked. His flashlight beam was shining on one of Sam's hands. Her hand was balled into a fist, and some long strands of something were hanging out. Sam looked down and opened her clenched fist. Wishbone came closer to get a better look. Draped over Sam's opened palm were three thin strips of leather.

"Buckskin!" Joe said. Wishbone could sense a note of fear in his voice. "Those look like the strips of leather that hang from buckskin clothing." Wishbone felt everyone's tension level rise. Everyone's gaze shifted slowly from Sam's outstretched hand to one another.

"What's going on?" said a voice behind them.

"Whowhatwhere!" Wishbone yelled, as he quickly spun around. He was about to bark at the intruder, until he saw it was only Rebecca. Everyone else was startled, as well. Four beams of light abruptly landed on the red-haired counsclor. She was standing there holding two soft-drink cans.

"What happened to you?" she said, staring at Sam, then at the others. She then looked to the docks. "And where's the tower?"

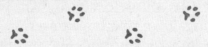

Someone watched the group of kids through the thick woods just off the shoreline of the lake. The rest of the kids were helping the one girl to her feet. The watcher tracked their movements as they all slowly helped the girl walk up the trail, heading toward the main road. The watcher

*parted the bushes to get a better look. The kids slowly
disappeared down the trail.*

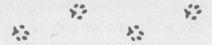

Sam sat in the camp office. She had stopped by
her cabin to change out of her wet clothes. She was
drying her hair with a towel as she looked around the
small room. Everyone except Barry and David were
there. Those two had gone to check on the campers.
Sam reached down and scratched Wishbone on the
head. Since the accident, he had stayed right by her
side. The dog's concern was comforting to her.

Everyone was silent until Mr. Alexander spoke up.
"Well, that settles it," he said. "Pranks and vandalism
are one thing." He looked over at Sam. "But now someone almost got seriously hurt—almost drowned, in
fact." His eyes went to the floor. "I'm so sorry, Sammy.
You could have died out there. I feel responsible."

"It's not your fault," Sam replied. She turned to
Rebecca. Sam couldn't keep her suspicions to herself
any longer. "Where were you the whole time,
Rebecca?"

"*What?*" A look of complete shock and surprise
spread across the counselor's face. "Are you accusing
me of knocking down that huge tower?"

"I don't know," Sam said. She wasn't sure about
anything anymore. "You were the last one there. You
also acted as if you didn't hear anything. The other
counselors and some of the campers heard the huge
splashing noise the tower made when it fell into the
water. But you did not."

"I was inside the food-storage locker," Rebecca replied. "I couldn't hear anything in there."

"It's true, Sam," Joe said. "She was still in the locker when Jeremy and I started to run to the docks."

"I'm sorry, Rebecca," Sam said. "It's just that you and Jeremy are always the last ones to appear on the scene right after something spooky happens."

"What are you trying to say?" Jeremy asked, as he looked directly at Sam. It was clear he was being defensive about being accused. "Are you saying *we've* been vandalizing the camp?"

"Now, kids . . ." Mr. Alexander interrupted. "There's no need to—"

Joe didn't let him finish. "Well, it's kind of true." He turned to face the others. "What about the campfire incident?"

Sam jumped back into the conversation. "Yes! And what about the muddy shoes you two were wearing?"

"We explained that," Rebecca answered. "We were working at the docks."

Sam didn't let that sway her. "It could have been mud from the docks. But it also could have been mud from around the lake's inlet." She turned to Mr. Alexander. "They could have cleaned away all signs of the campfire, then run around the bank of the inlet. That way, they could have run across the bridge and appeared as if they were coming from the other side of the camp."

"That's crazy!" Jeremy said angrily. He began to pace. Sam noticed that the office's door was open. David stepped in as Jeremy continued. "That 'campfire' was just something Joe imagined he saw."

"I don't think so," David said. Everyone turned to him. Sam noticed that David was holding a dark object in his hand. He held it up. "I found this hanging in the trees above the spot where Joe saw the campfire."

Mr. Alexander held out a hand. David gave him the object. Sam thought it looked like an old coffee can that had been spray-painted black. It had a wooden rod sticking through it. There was also some string or wire dangling from holes poked into the can. "This looks similar to the rig we used to create the smoke effect at the opening ceremony," the camp director said, as he turned the object over in his hands.

"That's what I thought," David said. "I don't think the campfire *was* just something created by Joe's imagination."

Jeremy and Rebecca looked at each other. "So," Rebecca said, "that doesn't prove that we had anything to do with it."

"What about the incident with the drumbeats?" Sam asked.

"Yeah. You two showed up conveniently late for that one, too," Joe added.

"Now, wait a minute . . ." Jeremy said.

David turned to Mr. Alexander. "There was something unusual about the beating-drum sound." David told them how he had heard a half-beat just after the drum had stopped beating. He explained how he thought it could easily have been two drums instead of one. "Both Jeremy and Rebecca arrived late after that, as well." David continued: "*Both* of them— as in *both* drums beating at the same time—could give

184

the impression of a ghostly drum sound floating through the forest."

Everyone turned to the brother and sister, expecting them to protest again. They seemed almost speechless. Sam noticed even Wishbone seemed to be waiting for some kind of reaction from the two. Finally, after an uncomfortable silence, Rebecca took a deep breath and spoke.

"Okay," Rebecca said. "We did it." Both she and her brother lowered their heads.

Jeremy spoke up. "We were just trying to get everyone into the spirit of the camp legend." He looked around the room. "We just wanted to give everyone a little scare."

Mr. Alexander looked very upset. "What about Sammy?" he said. "She could have been killed. Was that prank supposed to be just a *little* scare?"

Both Jeremy and Rebecca's eyes widened. "We didn't have anything to do with that," Jeremy said.

"We only did the campfire and the drum pranks," his sister added. "We didn't have anything to do with any of the vandalism!" They gazed around the room at all the staring faces. It didn't look as if anyone believed them.

"Really!" Jeremy pleaded. "We honestly thought Blue Bear was responsible for all the vandalism."

"I believe you," Sam said. Everyone turned to her in disbelief. "I think whoever it was that knocked down the tower was the same person who rescued me." Everyone looked at one another for a moment. Then Sam continued. "None of you could have done it, because the whereabouts for all of you were accounted for. The only person for whom there appears to be no alibi is Rebecca, and she wasn't wet when she arrived on the scene."

As everyone seemed to agree with Sam's theory, she looked down at her hand. She was still holding the three damp strips of leather. Sam knew it was none of the camp staff who had saved her. She wondered if it was the same person she had seen in the woods two days before.

Chapter Fifteen

Wishbone followed behind all the counselors as they walked down the main road toward their cabins. Mr. Alexander had already returned to his room, behind the main office. Wishbone thought the camp owner was going to sell the camp for sure now. They had discovered who had been behind the ghostly sightings. But the mystery of all the acts of vandalism and Sam's tower accident still remained unsolved. For the safety of the campers, Mr. Alexander was probably going to sell the camp to the men from Blue Bear the next day.

Mr. Alexander had invited the dog to stay at the camp so he could be its official guard dog. Wishbone felt he had let Mr. Alexander down in a big way. He had let everyone down, and Sam had almost gotten seriously hurt. Wishbone thought that guarding the Talbot house, back in Oakdale, was a lot easier than guarding a large summer camp. Maybe Mr. Alexander should have hired a professional guard dog, instead.

The counselors reached the first trail leading to the first set of cabins. Joe, David, and Jeremy turned left. Sam and Rebecca continued to walk toward the trail that led to their cabin. Joe stopped and turned toward the girls.

"Sam, wait up," Joe said. He ran to catch up with her. Sam stopped walking. Rebecca continued down the path. Wishbone stayed with Joe.

"May I borrow one of those leather strips?" Joe asked, as he pointed his flashlight at one of Sam's hands.

"Sure," Sam replied. She opened her hand and held out the three strips. Joe reached over and took one from her. "What do you want it for?" she asked.

"I have a plan," Joe replied. "I'll tell you about it in the morning. Right now, you should get some rest. You've been through a lot tonight."

Sam closed her hand over the remaining two strips of leather. "You're right," Sam said. "I'm beat." She turned and continued down the main road. "Just promise to tell me tomorrow," she said, without looking back.

"You got it," Joe answered. He and Wishbone watched as Sam turned left down the next trail, which led to the girls' cabins. "Come on, Wishbone," Joe said. "I have a plan."

As the two continued on the main road, Wishbone thought he might have an idea of what Joe's plan was. If he was thinking what Joe was thinking, that plan would be the perfect way for Wishbone to get back his original guard-dog status.

Joe and Wishbone reached the point in the road

where two trails forked off from it. They took the righthand trail, which led to the canoeing area. When they reached the docks, they walked over to where they had found Sam earlier that night. Joe knelt beside the spot.

"Here you go, Wishbone." Joe held out an open hand. The thin strip of leather stretched across his palm. "Let's put that extra-sensitive nose of yours to work."

"I won't let you down, Joe," Wishbone said with a wag of his tail.

The dog placed his nose over Joe's hand and took in a deep breath. The first thing he smelled was the lake water. Then the smell of wet leather filled his nostrils. Wishbone exhaled, then took in another breath. Lake water . . . Wet leather . . . And something else. Something familiar. Wishbone gave the strip a quick succession of sniffs. Sometimes that helped. This time it did. Wishbone identified the familiar odor as the one that he had been smelling all over camp.

He didn't recognize it at first because it was so strong. When he had come across that smell in the past, it had always been much weaker and much older. The dog had never been to summer camp before. He finally decided that the scent was one of those basic summer-camp smells. Now Wishbone knew that this smell belonged to someone who had been all around the summer camp. And that someone had been at the camp for a long, long time.

"You got it, boy?" Joe asked. "Can you track that scent?"

The terrier moved his nose from Joe's hand to the ground. The smell was there again. It was weaker, but Wishbone could definitely smell the same scent that was on the leather strip. He went over to the wooden posts that had supported the tower. The scent was there also. With his nose to the ground, Wishbone began to follow the scent trail down to the shore of the lake. The trail was leading away from the canoeing area and toward the old bridge. Wishbone came across the scent trails left by David and Barry as they had run to help Sam. He focused on the mystery smell, however. That scent belonged to whoever had tried to hurt Sam. Wishbone was going to find out whom the smell belonged to—if it was the last thing he did!

Joe watched as Wishbone took off down to the lakeshore. Joe was sure the dog was hot on the trail. He and Wishbone walked around the edge of the lake. Then Wishbone took a sharp left into some nearby bushes. As the dog seemed to linger in that area, Joe looked around. From the place Wishbone had led him, someone could have watched everyone as they were gathered around Sam. The person watching could also have been safe from being seen by David and Barry as they ran from the bridge toward the docks. Goose bumps began to form on Joe's skin as he thought of someone watching them while they had all gathered around Sam.

Wishbone sniffed the area a while longer. Then he

took off into the woods. The dog maneuvered more easily through the thick vegetation than Joe did. But Joe managed to keep up.

After a while, Joe realized that Wishbone was following a scent trail that ran right beside the path that led away from the docks and toward the main road. To move a little faster and easier, Joe made his way out of the woods and onto the actual trail. With his flashlight, he was able to keep tabs on Wishbone. The dog was following the scent with a lot of dogged determination. Sometimes Joe had to run just to keep up.

The two continued up the trail—one on it, and the other sniffing through the woods beside it. When they reached the main road, Wishbone continued to travel through the woods only a few feet away from the open road. Joe was starting to feel more uneasy than ever. He suspected that whoever had pulled Sam from the water had followed the group from the docks. Whoever it was had stayed in the woods, just off the main road.

Wishbone followed the scent trail all the way back to the camp's office. When he and Joe got there, what Joe was afraid would happen actually did occur. Wishbone tracked the trail to the back of the office. The dog looked up at the small window. Joe looked inside to see the very place where he and his friends had been only a half-hour before. It seemed that their mystery "guest" had been watching them there, as well.

Wishbone took off toward the parking lot. Joe followed close behind. His flashlight beam bounced as he ran. He followed the dog across the lot and into the woods on the other side. The woods were thick at first, but they thinned out a little as they hiked deeper into them.

As they made their way among the trees and bushes, Joe tried to get an idea where they were. At first he thought they were heading south. They seemed to be hiking parallel to the trail that led to the first set of cabins. Soon, however, Wishbone seemed to change their direction so that they headed southwest. He and Wishbone quickly came out from the woods and found themselves on the trail they were hiking next to. A quick look around told Joe that they had already passed the group of cabins.

From there, Wishbone ran down the trail itself. Joe was relieved to see that their visitor had decided to walk out of the woods for a while. Wishbone led Joe to the place where the trail made a sudden turn to the west. The dog, however, was following a different trail. Wishbone followed the scent trail in exactly the opposite direction. The terrier took a sharp left. Once again, he made his way through the thick woods. Joe ducked under a branch and followed his dog.

After slowly making their way through some unusually thick woods, Wishbone and Joe found themselves on another trail. This one seemed a little more overgrown than the camp's other trails. Nevertheless, it was definitely a hiking trail. This particular trail, however, hadn't appeared on the camp map.

Joe shone his flashlight on the trail ahead of him. Wishbone was sniffing around, almost in circles. It looked as if he had lost the scent. "Come on, Wishbone," Joe whispered. "Let's see where this trail leads. . . ."

Joe stopped talking when he noticed his flashlight beam begin to dim. He knelt down and examined it. The light flickered a little, then dimmed some more.

"Aww, come on!" Joe said, as he slapped the flashlight against his open palm.

The light flickered a bit brighter for a moment, then went out completely.

"Perfect," Joe muttered to himself.

Joe took in his surroundings. He hoped his eyes would adjust quickly to the dim light cast by the moon. Unfortunately, the thick forest spread a large canopy over the open trail. Not much light seeped in.

Suddenly, Joe heard a loud crunching noise. He froze. For a moment there was only the sound of a slight breeze and insect noises. Then there was another crunch. Joe felt a chill run down his spine. He shook his flashlight, but nothing happened. Then he heard another crunch. To Joe, the crunches sounded like footsteps on dried leaves. They sounded as if they were getting closer.

Crunch.

The noise *was* getting closer. Joe's heart pounded faster. He shook the flashlight again. It still didn't work.

Crunch.

Even closer yet. Joe really thought it had been a bad idea to go on this mission without the other counselors. He shook the flashlight again. Nothing.

Crunch.

Closer still. Wishbone began to growl. Joe's mouth was completely dry. A thick lump sat in the back of his throat.

Crunch.

Joe shook the flashlight even harder.

Crunch.

It refused to shine.

Crunch.

Wishbone growled a bit louder.

Crunch.

Crunch.

Crunch.

Joe slapped the malfunctioning flashlight as hard as he could. A bright beam of light shot from it. The beam landed on a figure standing in the middle of the trail only three feet away from them. Joe gasped as two large eyes lit up in the shaft of light. Startled, the deer leaped into the woods and bounded away.

Joe felt relieved, but not for long. His flashlight beam began to flicker again. "Maybe we should come back in the daylight," he told Wishbone.

Joe turned back, the way they came. As Joe made his way to the main trail, his thoughts roamed back to the camp's legend. Wasn't the ghost of Ka Nowato able to change himself into any animal? Joe decided it *would* be best to go back to that part of the camp only during daylight hours.

Chapter Sixteen

On Friday morning, Wishbone trotted beside Joe on the way back from breakfast. The dog had stayed close to Joe all morning. After their spooky experience the night before, Wishbone thought Joe could probably use some steady company. The terrier looked into the passing woods as they walked. Well, maybe Wishbone could use the company as well.

At breakfast, Joe had told Sam and David about the trail he and Wishbone had found, the one that wasn't on the camp's map. Everyone agreed to visit the mystery trail after lunch. Wishbone was glad he was going back to investigate in the daytime. He was also glad he would be traveling with a pack this time.

David and Sam left the cafeteria to get ready for their morning classes. As Wishbone and Joe made their way to the basketball court, Wishbone thought about the camp legend. The dog was no ghost expert. But he wondered if ghosts really had scents. All week, Wishbone had the feeling of being watched. When he had followed the scent trail the night before, he had realized that his feeling was true. Someone had been watching him and Joe. Someone had watched while they were with Sam on the lakeshore by the canoes. That same someone had followed them up the main road. Then that someone had watched them through one of the camp office's windows. The dog's fur bristled. It was one thing to have a feeling of being watched. It was an entirely different matter to discover that the feeling was true.

Overall, however, Wishbone was in a much better mood. His level of self-confidence was rising. The dog had actually helped track the vandal. Although he and Joe hadn't found out who it was, Wishbone was still glad he could be of help. Finally, he felt as if he was living up to his guard-dog title.

When he and Joe got to the trail leading to the basketball court, they saw Jack Conner. The young boy was standing just off the main road.

"Hi, Jack," Joe said. "You're a little early. Did you want to get in some extra practice?"

"Not exactly," the youngster said. Wishbone watched as Jack told Joe he had something else in mind.

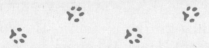

"Are you ready?" Joe asked. He checked Jack's harness. The two were standing high atop one of the towers at the confidence course.

"I think so," Jack replied. Both of his hands were holding firmly onto the top rope.

Joe looked down at Barry. The counselor was, once again, harnessed up and holding onto Jack's safety line. Wishbone stood beside him. He wagged his tail in anticipation as he watched Joe and Jack.

"When you get going," Joe said, "I'll climb down and go to the other tower. Remember, you have nothing to worry about. Barry will catch you if you fall."

"Okay," Jack said a little nervously. "I can do it. I know I can do it."

Joe thought the youngster was talking to himself more than he was to anyone else.

"All right," Joe said calmly. "Whenever you're ready . . ."

Jack took in a couple of deep breaths. He just stood there, looking toward the other tower. Joe thought that the other tower must have seemed a million miles away to the young camper. Jack took in another deep breath. For a moment, Joe didn't think the boy was going to move. Then, finally, Jack slid his right foot onto the outstretched rope.

"That's it, Jack," Joe said encouragingly. "You can do it."

The boy paused a moment, then shuffled his left foot closer to his right. He slowly slid his right hand out. His left hand soon followed, and Jack was no longer standing on the platform. The young camper took a quick look down. When he did, he wobbled for a moment.

"Don't look down," Joe said. "Just concentrate on the ropes." The boy slowly steadied himself and stopped wobbling. Joe saw the small beads of sweat drip off the boy's forehead. "You're doing great, Jack," Joe said.

After a few more deep breaths, Jack shuffled a little farther out. Joe knew that Jack wasn't the most skilled camper who had ever crossed those ropes. But, from the look on his face, he was definitely the most determined.

When the young boy had moved out a little farther, Joe unhooked his own safety strap. "I'm going to the other side now," Joe said. He began to climb down the ladder. "Remember, Barry has you covered. You're doing fine."

Joe climbed to the bottom of the tower. He looked up to see that Jack was almost halfway across.

"Looking good, Jack!" he called up to the boy.

Joe walked over to the other tower. Out of the corner of his eye, he saw someone approach. He turned and saw the rest of his morning basketball group. Joe looked up at Jack. The young boy was moving a little faster. His gaze was still fixed on the two ropes. Joe looked back at the other kids and put a finger to his lips, motioning for them to be quiet.

Joe climbed up the other tower. When he reached the top, he reattached his own safety strap. Joe turned his attention back to Jack.

"You're almost there," he told the boy.

Jack was moving even faster by then. He shuffled his feet across the bottom rope, while he quickly slid his hand across the top one. A small grin was growing on his face.

"A few more steps," Joe said.

With a huge smile, Jack quickly closed the gap and made it all the way across. When he stepped onto the tower's platform, both Jack and Joe were surprised as the campers who had watched the performance broke into applause and cheers. Joe looked over to see the senior counselor cheering, as well. Wishbone gave two loud barks, jumped up and spun around in the air, then barked again.

Jack waved to the kids in his basketball group. He looked at Joe and smiled.

"Great job, Jack!" Joe said, patting the boy on the back. "What made you change your mind?"

"You did, Joe," the young boy said.

"I did?" Joe asked, surprised. "What do you mean?"

"Well," said Jack, "I've been visualizing myself crossing the ropes over and over in my mind." He smiled as he spoke. "You are the one who taught me that," he said. "I couldn't have done it without you. Thanks."

"No problem," Joe said. "Now, let's go play some basketball."

"Great!" Jack said. "But there's one more thing."

"What's that?" Joe asked.

"Can I cross the ropes again first?"

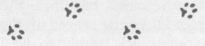

Wishbone sat on the wooden bleachers and watched Joe's morning basketball class. Joe didn't make the kids do any drills this time. He let the campers play a full game during the entire time class was in session. Wishbone enjoyed the game thoroughly. Most of his attention, however, was on only one player—Jack Conner.

201

It seemed that walking the ropes was not the only activity Jack had been visualizing. He was like a different person. He played with tremendous self-confidence and skill. Joe had been right. Jack did have the ability to play basketball well. He had just lacked self-confidence. Now, he seemed to have more than enough. The boy caught almost every pass that was thrown to him. More important, whenever he did miss a pass, he wouldn't let it upset him. He would just keep playing.

Wishbone wasn't the only one to notice the boy's transformation. Joe seemed to be amazed by his abilities. Even his teammates were shouting his name so they could pass him the ball.

"Way to go, Jack!" Wishbone barked from the bleachers. The dog thought the confidence course had done wonders for the young camper.

After practice, Wishbone and Joe walked toward the camp office. Since the camp owner hadn't been at breakfast that morning, Wishbone assumed Joe wanted to tell Mr. Alexander about the mystery trail. Maybe the camp's owner would know something about it.

When they reached the office, they found the front door open. Wishbone peeked his head in first. He didn't see Mr. Alexander. Wishbone *did* see a stranger. A gray-haired man in a faded blue sweater was standing in a corner of the room with his back to the door. He appeared to be rummaging through some of the cardboard boxes there.

"Who goes there!" Wishbone demanded in his deepest voice. He added a low growl for good measure.

The man spun around. His pale eyes were wide with

surprise. His thin face was covered in a short-cropped gray beard.

"Who are you?" Joe asked. "And what are you doing here?"

"You tell him, Joe," Wishbone said. "If he gives you any trouble, just say the word. There are plenty more growls where that one came from."

The man's eyes went from Joe to Wishbone and back. He stammered in surprise. "I . . . I just came to . . . to get the rest of my things," he said. "I'm Terrence Wells. I used to own this place."

Joe and Wishbone just stood there for a moment.

After a pause, the man pointed to some writing on one of the boxes. "See?" he said, pointing to the letters. "This is my name—T. Wells." He looked around nervously. "I called earlier. Mr. Alexander knew I was coming."

Wishbone slowly walked over to the man. "Let's check out your story, shall we?" The dog sniffed the man's pants legs. Then he gave a good sniff at the stack of boxes. Wishbone turned to Joe. "They are his boxes, all right, Joe," he said. "His story sniffs out."

"I'm sorry, Mr. Wells," Joe said. "I thought you might be someone else." Joe stepped forward and extended his hand. "My name is Joe Talbot. This is my dog, Wishbone."

Terrence Wells shook Joe's hand. He leaned down to pet Wishbone. "You gave me quite a fright there, Wishbone."

"Sorry, Terrence," the dog said. "Just doing my job."

The older man straightened up and looked at Joe. "Who did you think I might be, son?" he asked.

Joe looked toward the ground. He seemed a bit embarrassed. "No one, I guess," he said. "Someone has been pulling some pranks lately, and—"

Wells interrupted him. "Is that *still* going on?"

Joe's head shot up. "*You* had a prankster, too, when you owned the camp?" he asked.

"That's why I had to sell this place," the man said. "Those vicious pranks were extremely bad for business." Mr. Wells stepped over to the desk and sat in the chair there. "I'm too old to be chasing around after some silly joker. I thought Alexander would surely have put a stop to what was going on. Heck, I even gave him a great deal on the place. Sold it to him really cheap."

"Excuse me for asking," Joe said, "but didn't it upset you to have to sell the camp so cheaply?"

Wells leaned forward in the chair. His mouth tightened a bit as he gave Joe a sharp look. "You think I might be the prankster," he said, "don't you, son?"

"Well," Joe said, "some of us were just thinking—"

"Not mc, Joe Talbot," the man said. He leaned back in his chair.

Joe had a troubled look on his face. "What about Blue Bear?" Joe asked. "Couldn't you have gotten a much better deal from a big company like that?"

"If I thought Blue Bear was behind the pranks," the man said, "do you think I would give it the satisfaction of winning?"

"We think someone from Blue Bear may be responsible, as well," Joe said.

"If it is someone from Blue Bear," said Wells, "whoever it is is real slick. Like I said before, I could never catch the prankster."

Wishbone pawed the air. "Don't worry, Joe," he said. "This guard dog will come through. You'll see."

Joe gave a nervous laugh. "Maybe it's the ghost."

Mr. Wells laughed. "Do you mean Ka Nowato?"

"Where?!" Wishbone said, doing a full turn.

Mr. Wells continued. "Joe, I'm sorry to tell you, but there's no such thing as the ghost of Ka Nowato."

"What?" Wishbone asked.

"What?" Joe asked.

"That's right," Mr. Wells said. "I think the owner before me, the one who built this camp, made it all up. There was never any sacred burial ground, ancient warrior, or, as far as I know, a Chitowa tribe." He laughed a little. "That legend was just supposed to give the camp some character."

"None of it's true?" Joe asked.

"Oh, I'm sure some Native Americans lived in these woods at one time or another," the man said. "But I've never heard of the Chitowa."

Wishbone noticed a small smile come to Joe's lips. Mr. Wells must have seen it, too.

"What is it, Joe?" the man said. "You weren't actually falling for that old legend, were you?"

Joe let out a small laugh. Wishbone saw his friend's face turn a shade of red. "Well," Joe said, "I guess I did let myself get wrapped up a little."

"Oh, there's nothing to be ashamed about," said Mr. Wells. "That's what those old legends are for. But don't worry. Ka Nowato is just the product of someone's imagination."

Wishbone couldn't believe it. All that time he had believed there was a ghost of an ancient warrior watching over them. The camp's first guard dog felt a bit embarrassed. The dog thought a moment. If there was *no* ghost, then whoever had been pulling the pranks was definitely real. Wishbone's mind went back to the trail he and Joe had found the night before. The dog thought the answer to the mystery had to be there.

"Mr. Wells, what do you know about the trails that run along the southeast side of camp?" Joe asked.

Wishbone figured that Joe must have been thinking the same thing he did. After all, great minds thought alike.

"There's nothing special about them, I suppose," the man said. He got up and lifted the top box off of the stack. "Say, Joe, can you help me carry these boxes to my truck?"

"Sure," Joe replied. He took the box from Mr. Wells, and the man grabbed another one. Wishbone followed them as they stepped out of the office.

"The southeast side, huh?" Mr. Wells said. It seemed as if he were talking more to himself than actually asking someone else a question. "You know," he said, turning to Joe, "that was the part of the camp I was planning to expand."

The two made their way to the parking lot, and Wishbone followed closely. Mr. Wells and Joe set the boxes down in the bed of an old blue pickup truck. Joe and Wishbone followed the man as he headed back to the office to get another load.

"Business was really good before the pranks started," Mr. Wells continued. "I was going to add a whole group of new campsites in the southeast woods." He and Joe grabbed the two remaining boxes and walked back to the truck. "Other than that," the man said, "there is nothing special about that part of camp."

Mr. Wells closed the truck's tailgate and climbed into the cab. "It was nice meeting you two," he said. "Wish Tom good luck from me, and tell him I'm sorry I missed him."

Wishbone and Joe watched as the camp's former owner drove away. "Come on, Wishbone," Joe said. "I think it's time for lunch." Together, Wishbone and Joe started to walk down the main road. "And after lunch," Joe continued, "we can tell Mr. Alexander and the others the truth about the ghost of Ka Nowato."

Chapter Seventeen

"That was a good lunch," Wishbone said as he walked down the camp's main road. "Whether the camp is really haunted or not, this dog has to maintain his strength!"

Wishbone trotted behind Joe, Sam, and David. They all walked along with Mr. Alexander on the way to the camp office. Joe explained to Mr. Alexander about the scent trail Wishbone had followed, and about the mysterious trail they had found. Then Joe told everyone about the meeting he had had with Mr. Wells, the camp's former owner.

"So the story *isn't* true?" Mr. Alexander asked. The man seemed quite surprised.

"Apparently not," Joe said.

"You didn't already know that?" David asked Mr. Alexander.

"Not at all," he replied. "I just read the legend that was framed in the office. I assumed there *was* such a thing as the Chitowa tribe."

"So, there is no ghost of Ka Nowato," Sam said, "and someone had been pulling pranks long before you even owned the camp."

"I thought I had trouble bringing people in just because the camp had been closed for a couple of years and people had forgotten about it," Mr. Alexander said.

"Do you think Blue Bear was responsible for the pranks back then?" Sam asked.

"Except for what Jeremy and Rebecca did, I'll bet the same person is responsible for all of the pranks," David said, "whoever it is."

"Absolutely," Wishbone agreed. "I've smelled really old prankster smells all over the camp."

The group passed the trails that led to the basketball and confidence course areas. The camp office and parking lot came into view. "Well, I'm very sorry to say this, kids," Mr. Alexander said, "but when the people from Blue Bear get here, I'm pretty sure I'm going to take their offer."

"Oh, no!" Sam said, putting a hand over her mouth.

Mr. Alexander looked at her. "I'm about to be out of business, Sammy." He looked around and scratched his head. "I've finally lined up some more counselors, but I just don't have enough new campers coming in to keep this place running."

"It looks like Blue Bear has won," David said, disappointment in his voice.

"I'm not sure they are the ones responsible," Joe said. "I don't know how, but I think the answer has something to do with that trail we found."

As the group approached the camp office, Sam

tugged on Mr. Alexander's shirtsleeve. "Let us check it out for you," she said. "We may be able to solve this mystery yet."

"I don't know, Sammy," Mr. Alexander said. "If we haven't found out anything by now, it's probably too—" He stopped in mid-sentence. His gaze shifted from Sam to just over her shoulder. Wishbone looked over to see a shiny, black sedan pull into the parking lot. It was the men from Blue Bear.

Wishbone finished Mr. Alexander's sentence. "Too late."

Sam watched as the black sedan pulled to a stop. Mr. Alexander patted her on the back. "Thanks anyway, Sammy. It was worth a shot." He left the group of kids and walked over to meet the men from Blue Bear.

Sam felt terrible. She seemed to think she had personally let Mr. Alexander down. Her mind went back to what her father had told her. He had told her how their friends had all helped them when they were starting their own business. Sam and her father's friends helped get Pepper Pete's off the ground. That was why her father had sent her to Camp Ka Nowato. Mr. Alexander was a good friend, and she was supposed to help him. Instead, she felt she had let him down.

Sam's thoughts went back to the previous night. After her frightening experience, Sam couldn't sleep. She had picked up her Agatha Christie novel and read it to the very end. In *A Caribbean Mystery*, just as at Camp Ka Nowato, the mystery seemed to be impossible to solve. First, Major Palgrave had been poisoned because he had recognized a murderer. The maid, Victoria, had been killed next to help cover up the murderer's tracks. Then, soon after that, Lucky Dyson was found drowned.

Just as the kids had a prime suspect in Blue Bear, so did Miss Marple. To her, it seemed that all the evidence pointed to Greg Dyson, Lucky's husband. It was Dyson's heart pills that Victoria had found in Major Palgrave's room. They were put there to make it appear as if the major had heart trouble. Victoria was found murdered soon after she had found the pills.

When the major had spoken of the murderer to Miss Marple, he had told her a story about a husband murdering his wife. With Dyson's wife now dead, things looked even worse for him.

However, Miss Marple was not convinced. Something was nagging at her, but she didn't know what. Finally, it came to her, and she knew who the real murderer was.

Back before the entire mystery began, Major Palgrave had been telling Miss Marple story after story. One of those stories was about how the major had lost one of his eyes on an expedition. He now had a glass eye. Miss Marple realized that was a very important fact.

The major had also told her a story about the murderer. He had pulled a small photo out of the collection he carried with him. He was about to show her the photo when a look of recognition came across his face. He looked at the photo and then over Miss Marple's shoulder at a group of approaching guests.

One of the guests was Greg Dyson. It appeared to Miss Marple that Major Palgrave looked at the photo of the murderer and then recognized him in the approaching crowd. But Miss Marple didn't realize that she was looking at the major's glass eye. The glass eye *appeared* to be looking over her shoulder and toward the approaching guests. However, Major Palgrave was really looking a little farther over. He was looking at Tim Kendal. The major probably hadn't looked at that photo for quite some time. When he looked at it again, he noticed the murderer in the photo was sitting only a few tables away.

Tim Kendal was the murderer! He had killed the major and tried to make it look like a heart attack. When Victoria had come too close, he had killed her, as well. He had then killed Lucky Dyson by mistake. While she took a midnight swim, Tim Kendal mistook her for his wife. He had been planning to kill his wife all along, just as he had done to his two wives long ago. Major Palgrave knew of Tim Kendal's past crimes, but he had never caught him. Miss Marple hoped the major would have been pleased to know that Tim Kendal had been captured just before he could kill his third wife.

Sam's thoughts came back to the present. She had an idea. Miss Marple had solved her mystery by remembering a key piece of information that she had simply discarded before—Major Palgrave's glass eye. Sam wondered if there had been something she had missed in the camp's mystery.

She grabbed Joe's arm and led him to the nearby camp map. "Joe, show me where you found that trail." David and Wishbone followed them to the map.

"Right around here," Joe said. He pointed to the bottom righthand section of the map. Joe pointed to a spot in the woods. Sam reached over and placed a hand on the spot where Joe pointed. She slowly rubbed her hand across that part of the map.

"What are you doing?" David asked.

Sam didn't answer. She continued to feel the map. Then she found what she was looking for. She moved in for a closer look. She raised and lowered her head to look at the map from different angles. When she saw what she was looking for, she smiled.

"Hang on," she said. Sam left Joe, David, and Wishbone standing by the map. She ran to where Mr. Alexander and the two men from Blue Bear were walking toward the camp office.

"Mr. Alexander," she said, "I need to speak with you for a moment."

"Sammy," he answered, "can it wait?"

"It's very important," she said.

"Okay," Mr. Alexander told her. He excused himself from the men and followed Sam to the map. They approached a very confused-looking Joe and David. "What is it, Sammy?"

"Look at the map, Mr. Alexander," Sam said, pointing to the spot where Joe had found the trail.

"Those are supposed to be trees, Sammy," Mr. Alexander replied. "I know they are not the best drawings."

Sam grabbed the man's arm and placed his hand onto the southeast corner of the map. "Feel," she said, "right here." He rubbed his hand across the map and gave her a puzzled look. "It's the trail," she said impatiently. "Someone painted over it. If you run your fingertips over this spot, you'll feel a raised area." She watched as all three of the others moved their heads up and down. Even Wishbone cocked his head as if he were looking, as well.

"It's there," she emphasized. "Notice how it's been painted over? And look here." Sam pointed to a spot in the trees a little farther over. With her fingernail, she scraped at something small, sticking out from the map. "It's dried glue," she said. "When we first saw the map, a dried leaf was stuck to that old piece of glue." She looked at the others. "We didn't think anything of it then. But now you can see clearly that something used to be glued here." She moved her finger down the trail toward the piece of glue. "This southeast corner used to be part of the camp," she said. "Someone has just tried to hide it."

"Let's go find out what it is," David said. His eyes lit up with excitement.

"Yeah," Joe agreed. Even Wishbone barked and wagged his tail.

Sam turned back to Mr. Alexander. "I know the men from Blue Bear gave you until today to decide whether to sell the camp. Can you stall them?"

"I'll sure try," Mr. Alexander said. "But you kids will have to hurry."

That was all they needed. The three friends took off and ran down the main road. Wishbone followed closely. As they were leaving, Sam overheard Mr. Alexander speaking to the two men.

"Before I sell this camp to you, gentlemen," he said, "let me tell you a bit of its history. Have you ever heard about the legend of Ka Nowato?"

Chapter Eighteen

David watched as Wishbone took the lead. He, Sam, and Joe quickly ran behind the speeding dog. David didn't know how long Mr. Alexander could stall the men from Blue Bear. The kids had to find out if Joe's mystery trail led them to a clue to solving the mystery.

David wasn't too surprised to learn that the camp's legend was just that—a made-up story, with no truth to it at all. He had to admit, he was a bit relieved. With everything that had been happening, he was starting to let himself believe in the legend. Like everyone else, several times he had had the feeling of being watched. David believed that even the most scientific person would get a case of the creeps if he or she were put in a similar situation.

The kids and Wishbone soon reached the point where the trail took a sharp turn. "Is this the spot?" David asked.

"This is it," Joe replied.

"The woods look pretty thick here," Sam said.

"Well," Joe said, "here we go." He pushed some branches aside and stepped into the thick vegetation. Wishbone didn't wait to be asked. The dog jumped over a fallen log and disappeared into the greenery. Sam went next, and David followed.

The three counselors slowly made their way down the overgrown trail. Wishbone hardly seemed to have any trouble at all. He was small enough to pass easily without getting tangled in the many branches, vines, and thorns that reached out for his taller friends.

The trip didn't take long. Just when David was really getting tired of being stuck by thorns of all shapes and sizes, the thick vegetation disappeared. The four investigators found themselves standing on an open trail. It was narrow and overgrown, but it was definitely an improvement over what they had just walked through. David looked back in the direction from which they had come. The camp's trail was nowhere to be found. The thick vegetation hid it completely from sight.

"Come on," Sam said. This time, she took the lead.

The group of camp explorers followed the narrow trail as it twisted through the forest. As he walked, David was positive he smelled wood burning. When they turned the next corner, he realized where the smell was coming from.

The three kids and Wishbone stood in the middle of a large clearing. They all stared at a wooden cabin. It looked very similar to the other cabins spread throughout the camp. This one, however, was much bigger. It probably had more than just one room. A thin, white trail of smoke floated out of a large chimney.

On one side of the cabin, between two trees, David saw firewood neatly stacked. A large axe was sticking out of a nearby tree stump. On some low-hanging branches of another tree, clothes were hanging to dry. David wasn't very surprised to see that the clothes were made of buckskin.

The three kids took a few steps closer to the cabin. Wishbone was right behind them. Sam leaned closer and peered through one of the windows. "Someone is certainly living here." Sam pulled away from the window. "It doesn't look like anyone is home now, though," she added.

Wishbone was giving the place the sniff-over of a lifetime. Joe was peering through another window. David went over to where the buckskin clothes were hanging. He reached out a hand and touched one of the dangling sleeves. It was damp. It also had narrow leather strips like the ones Sam had been clenching in her hand after her accident at the lake.

"These clothes are still damp," David said. "I'm betting that whoever they belong to was the one who pulled you out of the lake last night." David noticed that Wishbone was sitting back, pawing the air with one of his front paws. The dog seemed to agree with David's theory.

David's remarks had caught the attention of Sam and Joe. All the kids looked at one another. Then Joe turned and looked back at the cabin. "I wonder where the owner is right now," he said.

David looked with concern into the surrounding

woods. "Whoever it is," he said, "is probably not very far away."

From only a few feet away, the watcher in the woods peered in silence through a thick growth of leaves as the three kids and the little dog snooped around the cabin. The watcher didn't know how the kids had managed to find the hidden trail and the hidden cabin. However, they hadn't discovered the watcher yet. Perhaps it was time they did. The watcher slowly and silently moved closer to the unsuspecting teenagers. Without a sound, the watcher continued to close the gap. It was time to settle things.

Wishbone gave the hanging buckskin clothing one final sniff. *That was the smell, all right,* he thought. It was the same scent the dog had uncovered all over the camp. It was also the same scent that he and Joe had been tracking the night before. Out of the corner of his eye, the terrier saw his three friends investigating the area around the cabin. Three figures were near the building, and one was at the edge of the woods. Wishbone hoped they could find what they were looking for.

The little dog suddenly froze. "Wait one minute," he said. "Three figures by the cabin . . . and one at the edge of the woods . . ." Wishbone muttered to himself. "One, two, three, four . . ." His head shot up. "*Four?!* That's one too many!"

Wishbone quickly aimed his sharp gaze at the figure standing at the edge of the woods.

"Whoa!" he shouted in surprise. The dog barked loudly at the fourth figure. "Who are you?!"

Wishbone heard Sam, David, and Joe gasp as they turned to see the man standing in front of him. The dog was barking at a very spooky-looking man. He was a tall, older man with long gray hair. His entire face seemed almost hidden by the mass of tangled gray hair that was his beard. He wore a buckskin shirt and pants similar to the clothes hanging on the tree branch. Piercing blue eyes stared out from his face.

"What are you doing here?" the man shouted in a loud, gruff voice. "You have no business here!"

The three kids were silent. They seemed frozen with fear. Wishbone, however, had a bone to pick with the man. The dog took a couple of cautious steps forward. He positioned himself between the kids and the man.

"Hey!" Wishbone barked. He followed up with one growl, for good measure. "No one scares my friends!" he said. "And, besides . . . Are you the one who's been messing with the camp's food supply?"

The old man looked down at Wishbone. "Now, hold on, little doggie," he said, "this is my place. I do all the growling around here."

Joe stepped forward. "What are you doing here?" he asked. Wishbone thought Joe was being very brave. He did hear a bit of hesitation in his buddy's voice, though.

"I *live* here!" the man said, glaring at Joe.

"Are you the one who's been pulling all the pranks at the camp?" David asked.

The old man tilted his head back and shot a sharp look at David. "Maybe I am. Maybe I'm not."

"I was almost killed by one of those pranks!" Sam said angrily, stepping forward.

Wishbone saw the man's face soften for a moment. It quickly took on its hard, unforgiving look again as he stared back at Sam. "You kids have no business being at that old tower after dark." The man's sharp expression started to fade. "I mean," he said, "the wood in the support beams was all rotted out." He looked at Joe and David. "It was a disaster just waiting to happen."

Wishbone looked from the man to the kids. They were all stone-silent. They just stood and stared as if they were statues. Wishbone looked back at the man. He stared at the kids a little longer, then looked at the ground.

"I never meant for you to get hurt," he said to Sam. "I was just trying to scare everyone."

Sam took a step closer to the man. "Why?" she asked the man. "Why would you want to scare everyone away?"

The strange man walked over to where the axe was sticking out of the tree stump. He reached down and pulled out the axe. Wishbone immediately became tense. He was relieved, however, when the man set the axe aside and sat on the old stump. The kids turned to face him.

"My name is William Elder, and I've been living here in these woods for a long, long time," the man said. "I was living here right after this camp was built." He stroked his long gray beard with one slim hand. "You see," he continued, "a long time ago, I wanted to get away from the world and all of its problems. I became sick and tired of what you would call 'civilization.'"

"I know the feeling, William," Wishbone agreed.

Mr. Elder continued. "A good friend of mine, Wayne Brantley, owned this camp and let me have this old ranger station as my very own." He pointed to the trail that Joe and Wishbone had discovered. "For privacy, I blocked the trail leading here, and Wayne removed any mention of it from the camp's map and records."

Wishbone stepped a bit closer. He was fascinated by the man's story.

"Anyway," the man continued, "I pretty much kept to myself all the time. None of the campers knew I was here, so everything was just fine." The man stopped stroking his beard and looked into the woods. "Unfortunately, I had lived such an isolated life that I had no idea Wayne had been killed in a boating accident. It was at least a year after his death when I found out the camp was owned by someone else."

"Terrence Wells?" Joe asked.

Mr. Elder looked back at the kids. "That's him," he said. "Anyway, after a bit of thought, I realized that what Mr. Wells didn't know wouldn't hurt him. I continued to stay away from everyone, and the campers never bothered me. Everything was like it had always been."

"Until Mr. Wells started to expand the camp," Joe said.

"That's right," the man replied, a bit surprised by Joe's quick analysis of the situation. "I see you kids have been doing a little detective work," Mr. Elder continued. "Anyway, I found out Wells was planning to enlarge the camp. And guess where he was going to add a whole new area of cabins?" He didn't give the kids a chance to answer. "Right here! Right where my home is." He paused for a moment. "I mean," he continued, "I knew I didn't have any legal right to the land I was living on. But I had been here much longer than he had. I wasn't about to give up what had become my home."

"So you tried to scare everyone away," Sam concluded.

Wishbone felt more of a sense of calm coming from the kids. It seemed that learning the truth had put them a bit more at ease.

"Of course I did," the man replied. "I took advantage of the camp legend." He looked down at his clothes and continued. "I always had a strong interest in the original inhabitants of our country. I had studied Native American lifestyles and beliefs long before I moved out to these woods. When I realized I might lose the adopted home and land I had grown to love, I felt the need to protect my special place and fight to stay here. So, among other things, in order to scare people away, I made a few tomahawk holes in the canoes so they couldn't be used. I would open the food-storage locker doors by removing the hinges and stack all the food neatly outside. Or I would just remove the food and scatter it throughout the camp. It was easy to bring old Ka Nowato to life."

"Opened the doors by removing the hinges, huh?" Wishbone said, his tail wagging at the creative idea of getting to a food source. "I'll have to remember that one."

Elder stroked his beard again. "You kids are very bright. When you came along, I knew I'd have to be even more creative in my attempts to drive you away. That's why I pushed the tower into the lake." Mr. Elder looked at Sam. "I had no idea that anyone was in there, though. I'm truly sorry for that."

"It was a terrible experience, but now I'm okay . . . I guess," Sam replied. "I was really more scared than anything."

"But why are you trying to frighten everyone now?" Joe asked. "Mr. Alexander just bought the camp from Mr. Wells. He's having a hard time just keeping the camp alive. There's no way he's even ready to think about enlarging the place. No one was coming close to finding you this time."

"I didn't want to take any chances," the man replied. "Besides, it's been nice having the camp vacant for a couple of years."

"What about Blue Bear?" David asked. "What are you going to do if the company buys this place?"

"Who's Blue Bear?" the man asked.

The kids explained to the man about Blue Bear and told him what the company's plans were for the camp's property.

"A resort?" the man said, startled. He stood up from the tree stump.

"There's no way you can keep this cabin hidden from Blue Bear if it buys the property," David added.

"Alexander can't sell this place to them," Mr. Elder said.

"Oh, no!" Joe said, his eyes opening wide. "The men from Blue Bear are at the camp office right now!" From the looks on everyone's faces, it appeared they had forgotten that fact, as well.

"We have to stop them! Mr. Alexander doesn't have to sell the camp!" Sam said. She turned toward the trail. The other kids began to follow her. Wishbone was in high gear to take off, too.

"Wait!" Mr. Elder said. "I can get you there really fast!" He pointed to a spot in the woods and smiled. "Remember, I know of a lot of shortcuts."

Chapter Nineteen

Wishbone ran close behind Mr. Elder as the man led the group down a very narrow trail. Joe, Sam, and David were close behind him. In almost no time at all, the trail had led them to the camp parking lot.

"That was a great shortcut," Wishbone said, as he shook a few leaves out of his fur.

"Oh, no!" Sam said when she came out from the woods.

Mr. Elder turned to her. "What's wrong?" he asked.

Sam pointed to the empty parking lot. "The men from Blue Bear are gone."

Wishbone looked at the large parking lot. Sure enough, the black sedan from Blue Bear was gone.

"We're too late," Joe said.

"Let's find out for sure," Sam said, as she took off toward the office. Wishbone and the others quickly followed her.

When Sam got to the office, she gave a couple of light knocks on the door, then entered. Wishbone quickly went inside and jumped into one of the office chairs. It seemed that Mr. Alexander had cleaned them up so the men from Blue Bear would have somewhere decent to sit.

Mr. Alexander was sitting at his desk, looking at some important-looking papers.

"Are we too late?" Sam asked.

"Almost," Mr. Alexander replied. "I was just looking over this contract the guys from Blue Bear left for me. They drove over to one of their other properties. They should be back soon."

"Well, don't sign that contract," Joe said, as he stood behind Wishbone. The dog turned around to see Joe and David enter the office. "Mr. Alexander," Joe continued, "we'd like you to meet the ghost of Ka Nowato."

Wishbone watched as a slightly embarrassed William Elder stepped into the office. He stood there with his shoulders hunched over.

Mr. Elder told his entire story to Mr. Alexander. Although the camp owner seemed somewhat sympathetic to Mr. Elder's situation and to the reasons he gave for what he had done, he was not happy at all about the older man's actions.

"Do you realize you almost killed Sammy, here?" Mr. Alexander said, as he stood from behind the desk.

Mr. Elder looked down at the floor. "I know it's a poor excuse, but I really didn't know she was in that tower. When I realized she was in there, I jumped into the water and pulled her out of the lake as fast as I could." He looked at the kids, then back at Mr. Alexander. The old man stood up straight. "I'm ready to take full responsibility for all my actions," he said. "You can call the police to have me arrested. I'll go peacefully."

"I *should* report you to the authorities," Mr. Alexander said. "Not only have you endangered the lives of my campers, but you have caused me to lose the camp!"

The kids looked at one another in shock. "But, Mr. Alexander," Joe said, "we've found the prankster! You don't have to worry about any more trouble." The other kids voiced their agreement.

"I'm sorry, Joe," Mr. Alexander replied. "I wish it were that easy, but it's too late. I was hoping the first few weeks this summer would give me the money to finish renovating the camp." He shot a brief glance at Mr. Elder. "But because of Mr. Elder, here, I'm now completely out of money. I can barely afford to keep this place open another day, much less another week." He sat back down and picked up a pen. "I have been putting off the inevitable. Now I have no other choice but to sell the camp to Blue Bear." He began to sign his name on the contract.

Suddenly, with more speed than Wishbone would have thought the man capable of, Mr. Elder reached out and grabbed the pen from Mr. Alexander's hand.

"Before you sign that, son," the older man said, "let me run something by you." Mr. Alexander looked annoyed, but he remained silent. "What if I offered to pay for all of the damage I've done?" Mr. Elder asked. He twirled Mr. Alexander's pen between his fingers.

Mr. Alexander shook his head. "I don't know."

"Plus," Mr. Elder added, "I'll invest the money to

renovate Camp Ka Nowato completely. What do think about that?"

Wishbone looked from Mr. Alexander to Mr. Elder, then back again. Mr. Alexander opened his mouth to speak, but then quickly closed it. A confused look spread across his face. "Wait a minute," the camp owner said, leaning forward in his chair. "If you've been living off the land all of this time, how can you have that kind of money?"

Everyone looked at Mr. Elder. Mr. Alexander had asked a good question. Mr. Elder smiled. "When I said I left civilization and gave up everything, I didn't really mean *everything*." He looked around at the surprised group. "You see," the older man continued, "before I decided to make a clean break from society, I was a successful businessman." He pointed a thumb over his shoulder. "I've got my life savings and retirement fund buried in glass jars all over these woods."

"Cool!" Wishbone said. "I bury important stuff,

too! Maybe sometime we could compare burying techniques." *I knew there was a reason I liked this guy.*

Mr. Elder twirled the pen some more. "I didn't become a success by not having backup plans."

Everyone looked at one another. They seemed surprised that the man they had found living alone in the middle of the woods had enough money stashed away to renovate the entire camp.

Mr. Elder held out the pen to Mr. Alexander. "Now, you can sign away the summer camp to that Blue Bear company." Mr. Elder leaned in a little closer. "Or you can become partners with someone who knows these woods better than anybody."

Mr. Alexander took the pen from the older man and stared at it. Then he raised his head and looked at all of the kids. They were waiting to see what he was going to do. The camp owner looked at the pen and the contract one more time. He then quickly tossed the pen over his shoulder and extended a hand to Mr. Elder.

"It's a deal, partner," he said.

Smiling, Mr. Elder grasped the younger man's hand in both of his and shook it happily.

"All right!" Wishbone said with a loud bark. "We did it! We saved Camp Ka Nowato!"

Mr. Alexander looked at the kids. "Thanks, kids," he said. "It looks like Sammy's dad sent me lifesavers, after all."

Chapter Twenty

Joe looked out a side window of Walter Kepler's minivan. Mr. Kepler was driving him, Sam, David, and Wishbone to Camp Ka Nowato. It was a Sunday afternoon, several weeks after they had left the camp. Today was the beginning of Ka Nowato's last week of summer camp. Mr. Alexander had invited them all to come for the *official* opening ceremonies.

As Mr. Kepler turned left onto the narrow asphalt road leading to the camp, Joe thought back to the first week of summer. He and his friends had had quite an experience as counselors.

"Look," Sam said. Joe looked up from the back-seat. Sam was pointing at the road ahead. David and Joe leaned forward to get a better view. Even Wishbone seemed to see what Sam was pointing at.

Stretched over the road ahead was Camp Ka Nowato's welcome sign. It was the same wooden sign they had seen the first time they had come to the camp. It was still hanging from between two large totem poles. This time, however, both the sign and the poles were brightly painted. They had received a complete makeover.

Joe noticed an even bigger change. The bushes and trees along the roadside were neatly trimmed back. Freshly mowed green grass covered the road's shoulders. The smaller totem poles that greeted people were no longer tangled with vines. They all stood proudly, displaying fresh coats of paint.

Mr. Elder had agreed to pay all the costs of the renovations to the camp. Joe soon realized that the painted signs were only the tip of the iceberg.

When Mr. Kepler pulled the minivan into the camp's parking lot, Joe thought it looked like an entirely different place. New asphalt covered the parking lot. There were no weeds or grass poking out of cracks, the way there had been before. Even the forest surrounding the lot looked better. Joe realized he actually could see a distance into the woods. It seemed as if many of the twisting vines and thorn bushes had been cleared out. The forest now looked friendly and cheerful.

Walter slowed the van to a stop. He parked directly in front of the camp's office. The small building seemed to have undergone a complete change. It had a new roof, and it was covered in a fresh coat of paint. A large bay window had been built into the front of the office. From where Joe was, he could see a clean office inside. David opened the sliding side door and everyone got out.

"Wow!" Sam said. "This whole area looks totally different."

"This looks great," Walter said, as he looked around. "From what you told me, it used to look quite run-down."

"Before, it actually looked kind of spooky," Joe said.

"Now it looks great," David added.

The entire group walked toward the camp office. But something was wrong. It seemed empty. It made everyone remember how they felt on the first day they had arrived there to serve as counselors. They turned away from the office and walked across the empty parking lot.

"Sam?" Mr. Kepler said. "We were supposed to come *today*, right?"

"Today's the day," Sam replied. She looked around the empty lot.

As the group walked back to the office, Joe saw two people walk past the bay window and open the door. It was Mr. Alexander and Barry. They came out of the camp office.

"Hey, everyone!" the camp owner said. "How are my favorite lifesavers doing?" He shook everyone's hand.

"Well, Tom, since you haven't come to Oakdale to visit me," Mr. Kepler said, "I decided to come visit you." He shook Mr. Alexander's hand. "Hello, fellow businessman! How are you doing?"

"I'm great. Thanks for coming, Walter," Mr. Alexander said. He introduced Barry. Then he raised his arms, gesturing toward the camp. "What do you think of the place?"

"What I see looks great," Walter said. "The kids,

more than I, can see exactly how much hard work you've put into renovating the camp."

"You'd better believe it!" Mr. Alexander replied.

"Mr. Alexander," Sam said, "where is everybody?"

The man seemed as if he was about to answer her, but then he put a finger over his lips. He looked toward the main road. Everyone followed his gaze. At first, Joe didn't see or hear anything. Soon, however, he detected the faint sound of children singing. Then the noise began to grow louder. Next, Joe saw the shiny grille of a blue school bus. As the bus came closer, it was clear it wasn't alone. Almost right behind it came a parade of three other identical-looking buses. Soon, all four of the camp's buses pulled into the parking lot. They had all been freshly painted, and each was loaded with campers.

"I'll be just a moment," Mr. Alexander said, as he started to walk toward the parking buses. "I have some campers to get situated."

Everyone watched as the buses parked side by side. There was enough room left between them for each to unload its passengers and baggage comfortably.

As the group watched the buses park, Barry turned to face the kids. "I want to thank you again for what you did," the counselor said. "With all the problems we had at the beginning of the camp's season, I was thinking about finding another summer job." He looked at the row of buses. "But, since the situation got solved, I've ended up having the best summer ever." Barry looked back at the buses for a moment, then turned toward Joe and his friends. "Say, do you want to help us get everyone settled in?"

Mr. Kepler and the kids agreed, and they all followed Barry to the row of buses. Joe looked at the four bright blue buses. Dozens of cheerful campers were getting off the buses and waiting for their luggage to be unloaded.

As the passengers poured out of the large buses, Joe saw a couple of familiar faces. Wearing light blue Camp Ka Nowato T-shirts, Rebecca and Jeremy were lining up all the campers into several rows. Other counselors Joe didn't recognize were handing down the luggage from the buses' roofs.

To Joe, it seemed that the process of unloading the campers this time around was much more orderly and efficient than it had been the first week. Then, again, Joe figured Mr. Alexander and the others must have had plenty of practice by now.

Joe and his friends greeted Jeremy and Rebecca. Joe and Wishbone were about to help them with the kids when he felt a tug on his shirtsleeve. Joe turned

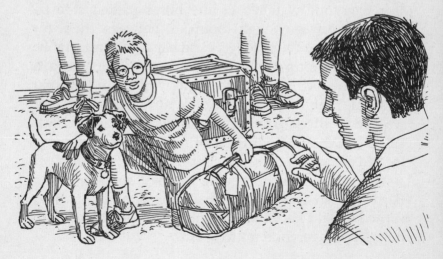

around to see Jack Conner. The young boy was holding a large duffel bag.

"Jack," Joe said, "what are you doing here?"

"I talked my parents into letting me come back for another week," the young boy said.

"That's great!" Joe said. "How are you doing with basketball?"

"A lot better," Jack said. "Thanks for helping me."

"You were already good," Joe told him. "You just needed to find your self-confidence. That's all."

Seeming to agree, Wishbone waved at the air with one front paw. Jack reached down and scratched the dog's head. He then looked back at Joe. "Are you going to be coaching basketball this week?" Jack asked him.

"No. We're just visiting."

"That's too bad," the youngster said. "You are a really great camp counselor." The boy slung the straps of his bag over his shoulder. "Thanks again," he said, as he moved off to join the other campers.

Joe smiled. He knelt down and scratched Wishbone behind the ears. Joe was glad he could make that kind of an impression on the young camper. Joe thought his father would have been proud. Joe had helped the young boy the same way his father had helped him once. Who knew? Maybe one day Joe could be a basketball coach just like his father.

Once all the campers had gotten off the buses, they were taken to their cabins. David and his friends split up. They each joined current counselors and groups of campers. David went with Jeremy and they led a group down the main road. This time, Jeremy did more than just show Joe and the others the camp's map. Jeremy gave David and the group of campers a real tour of the facilities.

David thought the entire camp looked great. There were still a few areas that had not been fully renovated. But most places showed a definite improvement. The basketball court, the confidence course, the pool, the archery range—all of those areas showed little resemblance to the way they had once looked.

There were new picnic tables and benches in the cafeteria. The stables had been completely rebuilt. David saw that Scout and Silver now had three other horses to keep them company. The whole dock area looked great. Dozens of new canoes were resting against large racks. David also saw a new, almost-finished safety tower. A half-finished roof sat atop a bright, unpainted tower.

As they continued the tour, David thought about his first week of summer camp. Like the others, David really had had a great time at Camp Ka Nowato. He had enjoyed the activities and helping out the young kids. He had even enjoyed taking a short break from technology and getting back to nature. There was even the possibility that he could work at the camp again the following summer. David wondered if, by then, he would have a laptop computer to bring with him. After all, there was roughing it, and then there was roughing it.

The group walked back to the main road. David was then surprised to see that Jeremy was leading this particular group of campers to the campsite across the old bridge. To David's added surprise, the old bridge wasn't there anymore. A new, wider bridge now stretched across the small inlet of water.

Jeremy and David led the campers across the bridge and into the campsite. Like almost everything else at the camp, the cabins had been completely restored. Once Jeremy assigned each of the kids to a cabin, he walked over to David.

"Listen," the red-haired boy said. "I'm sorry Rebecca and I scared everyone with those pranks and stuff." He looked down at the ground.

David looked at Jeremy. He was sure that it had been difficult for Jeremy to find the courage to apologize like that. "That's okay," David said. "I know that the campfire trick at the opening ceremony was not a prank, and it sure looked pretty cool." He looked around the campsite. "If you want, maybe later we can come up with some new chemical compounds. I'll bet there are all kinds of special effects we could create to use at camp ceremonies."

Jeremy looked up at David and grinned. "You really want to?"

"Sure," David said with a small laugh. "Even though Ka Nowato's existence isn't real, you should keep the legend alive. It's an important part of the camp's history."

Jeremy agreed.

After Sam went on a camp tour with Rebecca, she

entered the camp's ceremonial council ring. Even that area looked as if it had been spruced up. The benches and stage looked brand-new. A fire was burning on a large stone platform, just behind the stage, exactly the way it had during the week when Sam served as a counselor. This time, however, on each side of the platform there were two giant totem poles reaching toward the sky. They were by far the biggest totems in the camp. Sam thought they were a great addition to the council ring.

Sam took a seat on one of the benches and sat there and looked at the beautiful Native American carvings. Her mind drifted to the camp legend, and she thought about how Mr. Elder had used the legend to try to scare everyone and shut down the camp. Sam thought about all the renovations she had seen. It was as if Camp Ka Nowato was a completely different place. Sam thought it was ironic that the person who had tried to ruin the camp was the one responsible for eventually saving it and assuring that it would be there for years to come.

Soon, Sam was joined by her dad, David, Joe, and Wishbone. They sat on the bench next to her. Everyone discussed how the camp had improved since they had first been there. Sam's dad was very impressed. Everyone thought that Mr. Alexander and Mr. Elder had done a fine job restoring Camp Ka Nowato.

As Sam and her group spoke to one another, the counselors and campers began to file in and take seats. Sam wondered if she and her companions would see Mr. Elder that night. She wondered if he still kept away from everyone and lived like a hermit. Maybe he was still back at his cabin in the far reaches of the camp. Sam laughed as she thought maybe Mr. Elder was the ultimate silent partner.

"Hello, kids."

Sam turned around to see William Elder standing behind her. The older man looked much as he had the first time Sam and her friends had met him. He still wore a buckskin shirt and pants. His hair and beard seemed different—a little shorter and neater, maybe. The big difference, however, was in his expression and tone of voice. A friendly smile graced his lips. His eyes seemed kind instead of piercing. He spoke softly, instead of gruffly.

"What do you think of the new and improved camp?" he asked. "We have really been working hard these past few weeks."

"We think it's great," Sam answered. Everyone else voiced their agreement.

The man sat down on a bench next to Sam. Wishbone hopped down and went over to greet him. Mr. Elder patted him on the head. "How's that guard dog doing?" he asked the dog.

Wishbone wagged his tail and gave a small bark in reply.

Mr. Elder turned to the rest of the group. "Well," he continued, "you all will be interested to know that I don't keep to myself as much anymore." He looked around at the gathering campers. "Yup, Tom talked me into teaching the campers classes on living off the land and Native American folklore." He patted Wishbone on the head a few more times. "I teach right at my

241

cabin. I opened up the old trail to give everyone easier access to my quarters."

"That's great, Mr. Elder," Joe said.

"Yeah," David agreed. "I bet the kids get a lot out of your classes."

"They're not the only ones," Mr. Elder replied. "I get a lot out of what I do, too. I'm having a great time. I should have done this years ago."

Mr. Elder looked around at the gathering crowd. Sam followed his gaze. It seemed that almost everyone was there. Mr. Elder turned back to Sam.

"Sam," the man said, "you'll never know how badly I feel about almost hurting you that night at the lake." He reached for something that was around his neck. "I can never apologize enough. But there is something I want you to have."

Sam watched as he lifted a leather strap that was looped around his neck. An object dangled from the middle of it.

"I found this the first night I ever spent here at Camp Ka Nowato," the man said.

Sam saw that a small arrowhead was attached to the leather strip.

Mr. Elder held it out to her. "I've kept it ever since." The older man lowered the necklace over Sam's head. "Now I want you to have it. I want you to believe that I am truly sorry."

Sam held up the ancient arrowhead. "I don't know what to say. Thank you very much."

"Who knows?" Mr. Elder said. "Maybe that arrowhead belonged to Ka Nowato himself." He gave a quick wink to Sam, and everyone laughed.

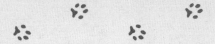

"Ah," Wishbone said. "Now, this is the way a summer camp *should* be." Wishbone looked around at all the happy faces. The light from the council ring's campfire danced across them. Wishbone sighed. The dog believed he could finally do what he had wanted to do the first time he had come to the camp—relax. Wishbone no longer needed to be head of camp security. There was no prankster to worry about. There was no ghost to worry about. He could just kick up his paws and enjoy the great outdoors.

While Wishbone had been away at camp, he realized how much he had missed his hometown of Oakdale. Sure, there was some noise and traffic there. And sometimes not everyone watched out for The Dog. But it was good to know that, back at Oakdale, Wishbone was the *only* one doing all the watching.

Wishbone watched as Jeremy and Rebecca left their seats and walked down toward the stage. Once again, they began to beat the two drums. The dog recognized the sound right away. Wishbone was sure those were the same drums the two kids had used when they were trying to scare everyone.

Once the two counselors started to beat the drums, the low murmur of the campers' voices stopped. Soon, all that could be heard were the deep drumbeats.

"That's right," Wishbone said, as he wagged his tail. "Put those drum skills to good use."

Wishbone turned around to see what he knew

was coming. He looked up to see Tom Alexander slowly walk down one of the narrow aisles. Once again, the man was dressed as a Native American chief. He made his way to the stage, walking in time to the drumbeats. When he reached the stage, Mr. Alexander put his hands up, and the drums stopped.

As he had done early that summer, Mr. Alexander told the story of Ka Nowato and the Chitowa people. Wishbone liked that story, even if it was only a fantasy. The story still taught everyone to be good to nature. That was a very important point. The story also told everyone about a great watchdog. Wishbone liked that, as well.

Soon, Mr. Alexander got to the part of the story where he would raise his arms high into the air. When he did that, a cloud of smoke would burst from the fire behind him. That was what had happened earlier in the summer. This time, however, when Mr. Alexander raised his arms, a large blue flame burst from the fire. All the campers gasped at the special effect. Wishbone thought it was great, as well. It was just like the one that had spooked him and Joe at the campsite across the bridge. Wishbone thought Jeremy did a really great job this time. That was much better than the smoke.

After Mr. Alexander finished the story of the legend, he welcomed everyone to Camp Ka Nowato the same way he had done before.

"I do have a special announcement to make this evening," the camp owner said. "I want to introduce some very special guests. If it wasn't for them, Camp Ka Nowato wouldn't be open this evening." Mr.

Alexander introduced Joe, Sam, and David. The audience applauded.

"Hey!" Wishbone barked. "Don't forget the dog!"

"And, of course," Mr. Alexander continued, "I'd like you to meet a guard dog that would make Ka Nowato himself very proud. . . . Wishbone!"

Wishbone wagged his tail with pride and joy. "Why, thank you, thank you!" The dog hopped off the bench, faced the campers, and took a small bow. "No, really. You're too kind." The audience laughed and applauded again.

After everyone had quieted down, Mr. Alexander continued. "Now, if you will all please follow your assigned counselors, they'll take you to your cabins. And, once again, welcome to Camp Ka Nowato!" The audience clapped again, then started to file out of the council ring.

Mr. Alexander made his way to where Mr. Elder, Wishbone, and his friends were sitting. "Thanks for coming, everyone," the man told them. "And I really meant what I said onstage. I have you to thank for all of this."

"I thank you, too," Mr. Elder added.

"We really had fun," David said.

"Yeah," Joe agreed. "Do you think you might need some counselors next summer?"

"I'll second that!" Sam added.

"And I third it!" Wishbone said, his tail wagging.

Mr. Alexander and Mr. Elder looked at each other, then back at the kids. "You bet," Mr. Alexander told them. "We'll put in a good word for you."

"We know the owners," Mr. Elder added.

Everyone laughed.

Mr. Alexander looked over and saw Jeremy following his group out of the ring. "Hey, Jeremy!" Mr. Alexander called.

Jeremy stepped away from his group and ran over to join Wishbone and the others.

"Great job with the fire tonight," Mr. Alexander said. "That blue flame was a nice touch."

"Absolutely," Mr. Elder added. "But I thought we weren't going to do the fire trick tonight. I thought we were fresh out of flash powder."

"We are," Jeremy said. A confused look was growing on his face.

"Well, then, what did you use?" Mr. Alexander asked.

"I didn't use anything," Jeremy answered. "I thought *you* did the fire this time." For a moment, everyone looked around at one another. An uncomfortable silence followed.

"Uh . . ." Wishbone said.

"Jeremy!" Mr. Alexander said. "Come on, now. Seriously, what did you use?"

"I didn't use anything—honest!" the counselor said. "The drop rig isn't even up in the tree." Jeremy shone his flashlight beam into the tree branch that hung over the tree. There was nothing there.

"So, Jeremy," Wishbone said, "if *you* didn't make the big scary blue flame, then *who* did?"

Everyone was looking at one another in confusion. It appeared that nobody had an answer for what had just happened. Mr. Alexander started to chuckle. Mr. Elder joined him. Slowly, one by one, everyone else began to laugh, as well. Soon, the entire group was caught in a round of belly laughs.

While they all laughed, Wishbone looked back toward the burning campfire. "Maybe there's another prankster in the camp," the dog said to himself. The fur on the back of his neck began to stand on end. "Then, again," he continued, "maybe there really *is* a ghost of Ka Nowato."

About Michael Anthony Steele

Michael Anthony Steele, or Ant, as he is known to his friends, went away to summer camp many times when he was a youngster. As an Eagle Scout, Ant camped at the George W. Pirtle Scout Reservation near Carthage, Texas. In fact, it was his experiences at Camp Pirtle that helped Ant create his first WISHBONE Super Mysteries title, *The Ghost of Camp Ka Nowato*.

Ant can relate to Joe's fears. In fact, Ant knows firsthand how it feels to be alone in the dark woods without a working flashlight. He also knows that a deer's footsteps on dried leaves can sound a lot like human footsteps. Of course, an active imagination helps them sound similar, as well.

During the second season of the WISHBONE television show, Ant worked as a staff writer and received the opportunity to cowrite the one-hour Halloween special, *Halloween Hound: The Legend of Creepy Collars*; the TV episode *War of the Noses*; and Wishbone's first movie, *WISHBONE's Dog Days of the West*.

His other credits include the WISHBONE Mysteries title *Forgotten Heroes,* The Adventures of Wishbone title *Digging to the Center of the Earth,* and the script for the CD-Rom, *Wishbone Activity Zone.*

Currently, Ant lives in Texas with his wife, Becky, and a houseful of animals. They have two Chihuahuas, named Juno and Echo; a Staffordshire terrier named Odessa; and an English bulldog named Rufus. Ant and Becky also have two Siamese cats, named Pluto and

Bromius; a snake, named Bishop; and an aviary full of finches and canaries. If Ant and Becky ever decide to take their entire family of animals camping, they had better bring along a *big* tent.

Coming Soon!

#16

WISHBONE
Mysteries

THE SIRIAN CONSPIRACY

By Michael Jan Friedman and Paul Kupperberg

The WISHBONE Mysteries #16

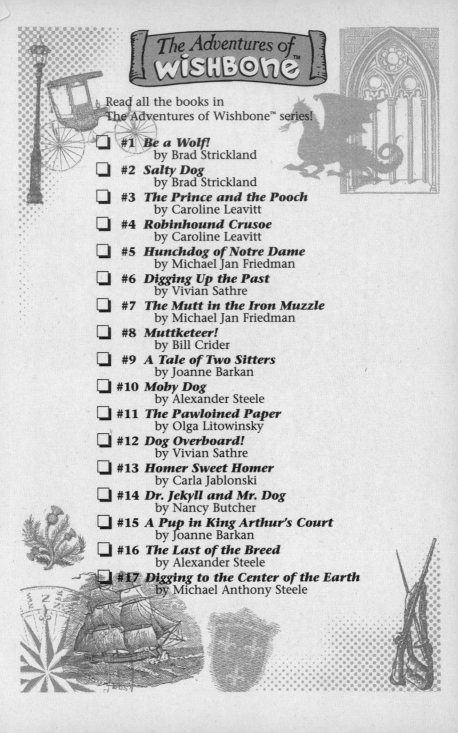

The Adventures of WISHBONE™

Read all the books in
The Adventures of Wishbone™ series!

The WISHBONE™ Super Promotion
*Free Wishbone™ Plush Dog or WISHBONE book!

Mail this form (or a reasonable facsimile), along *with proof of purchase of one WISHBONE book (original store-identified receipt dated between May 1, 2000, and December 31, 2000) to receive either a free Wishbone plush dog or WISHBONE book. This offer is only available while supplies last.

Please complete this form and mail, along with proof of purchase, to:
WISHBONE Super Promotion
Lyrick Studios
Attn: Marketing Manager
2435 N. Central Expwy. Suite 1600
Richardson, TX 75080-2734

PLEASE PRINT

Name_____

Address_____(NO POST OFFICE BOXES)

City _____ State _____ Zip _____

Please indicate your first and second choice of plush toy or book by printing "1" or "2" in the appropriate box:

[ ] Plush toy   [ ] Book

Terms and conditions:
Offer expires December 31, 2000 (responses must be postmarked by December 31, 2000). Limit one plush toy or book per person, family or household. Offer good only in United States and is void where prohibited. Employees and members of their families of Big Red Chair Books™, Lyrick Publishing, Big Feats Entertainment, L.P. and Lyrick Studios, Inc. (collectively "Companies") and their affiliates are not eligible. Requests will not be mailed to P.O. boxes. Companies are not responsible for late, lost, illegible, incomplete, postage-due, damaged, mutilated or misdirected requests or mail. Photocopies of purchase receipts will not be accepted. No exchanges. Offer good while supplies last. Companies make no representation regarding, and shall have no liability in connection with, the quality or use of the plush toy or book. If first choice is not available, second choice will be sent. Allow 6 to 8 weeks for processing from receipt of order.

SADDLE UP FOR A ROOTIN', TOOTIN' VIDEO ADVENTURE!

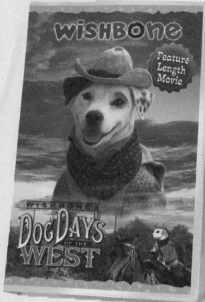

Wishbone™'s first feature-length movie!

No one in Chaparosa, Texas, knows how to tame the land better than Long Bill Longley (Wishbone). But, can he tame the town troublemaker and still hold off a big-city bank examiner? In Oakdale, Wishbone must help Wanda keep her good reputation when a sneaky reporter tries to paint her as the town tyrant. It's over 90 minutes of tumbleweed chasin', tail waggin' fun based on the short stories of O. Henry. See it only on home video. Read the WISHBONE™ book from Big Red Chair Books™

Available wherever videos are sold.

WISHBONE Mysteries

Read all the books in the
WISHBONE™ Mysteries series!